BEAR REIGN

ALPHA GUARDIANS - BOOK SIX

KAYLA GABRIEL

GET A FREE BOOK!

JOIN MY MAILING LIST TO BE THE FIRST TO KNOW OF NEW RELEASES, FREE BOOKS, SPECIAL PRICES AND OTHER AUTHOR GIVEAWAYS.

http://freeshifterromance.com

Bear Reign: Copyright © 2019 by Kayla Gabriel

ISBN: 978-1-7959-0217-5

All Rights Reserved. No part of this book may be reproduced or transmitted in any form or by any means, electrical, digital or mechanical including but not limited to photocopying, recording, scanning or by any type of data storage and retrieval system without express, written permission from the author.

Published by Kayla Gabriel
Gabriel, Kayla
Bear Reign

Cover design copyright 2019 by Kayla Gabriel, Author

Images/Photo Credit: Period Images

This book has been previously published.

AN EXCERPT

He didn't wait for a response, heading down a grand sandstone staircase and tugging his shirt off as he went. He stripped down to his boxer briefs, uncaring whether Sophie got an eyeful or not. He was overwhelmed and raw right now, he couldn't worry about her right now.

Shouldn't worry about her at all, in fact. Therein lay the problem.

The water was the perfect temperature when he dove in, just this side of refreshing. The sun had warmed the top and left the deeper recesses crisp and cool, and just the feel of the water on his skin was like sucking in a life-saving breath just when he felt he was drowning.

He did a dozen laps, slow and methodical, the exercise burning his tired muscles but acting as a balm for his overwrought mind. It was meditative for him, and he slipped so far into his own world that the sound of splashing water jolted him mid-stroke.

Ephraim surfaced to find Sophie wading in, wearing what looked like nothing but one of his t-shirts. The thin cotton was already damp around her breasts and hips, clinging to the slick outlines of her curves.

There went his meditative state. His whole body tightened, cock growing hard in an instant as he watched her approach. She gave him a self-conscious smile and dove under the surface, swimming over to come up just a few feet from him, treading water.

"Sophie…" he warned. "I don't think you want to come any closer. I'm on edge right now."

PROLOGUE

*E*phraim stood on a rocky bluff that overlooked the valley where his village lay, his long dark hair whipping wildly around his shoulders. He straightened his spine as he stared at the far mouth of the valley, watching as a line of a dozen of his village's warriors approached, returning from battle. Though Ephraim couldn't see their expressions from this distance, their movements were slow and heavy, almost defeated.

Or perhaps that was just his imagining. After all, it was hard to notice anything about the warriors in contrast with the burden they carried, a shrouded body lying on a pallet of cloth and heavy branches.

Ephraim's father, a fellow warrior fallen in a raid against a neighboring tribe.

Watching the warriors, with their tall frames and broad shoulders, always made Ephraim strain to stand up taller, to make himself seem older and stronger. At fourteen, he held himself up to the standard of his father and the other village heroes. His brothers Elias and Egrel, older than him by more than a decade, constantly tormented him about his lithe frame. It seemed nothing ever changed between them: Elias the rugged warrior, Egrel the clever sorcerer, and little Ephraim who would never grow into his clumsy feet and fierce angst.

Maybe you'll never mature, you'll just cling to mother's skirts all your life, was Egrel's newest taunt.

Ephraim realized that his fists were clenched tightly, just thinking about it. His father always told him to ignore Egrel's sharp tongue and Elias's quiet condescension, but it was difficult. It always seemed like his brothers bore some grudge against Ephraim, as if their brotherly teasing was something more. Something deeper, uglier.

Turning his focus back to the procession of warriors below, Ephraim knew the tension with his brothers grew out of competition. Ephraim was most beloved of his mother, and he'd inherited more than just his father's dark good looks — he also had the ability to shift into a great, furred beast. It was the same gift that had carried his father through a lifetime of sprawling, epic battles. The ability that had raised their family's status, given them the best of the valley's land to farm, given them a great number of sheep and cattle.

One day, Ephraim was destined to follow in his father's footsteps, become a respected warrior. Neither Elias nor Egrel could rely on such an ability to earn their keep, though Elias was talented with a sword and Egrel adept with potions and spells.

"Have they brought him, then?"

Ephraim whirled and found his mother standing at the

doorway of their cottage, leaning against the frame for support.

"Here, mother, let's get you back inside," Ephraim said, crossing the yard to assist her.

"That was your father, was it not? He wears the shroud," his mother mumbled. She was light as a feather when Ephraim half-carried her back to the makeshift bed they'd set up by the fire. The nights were cool this time of year, and her health was poor. Worse, even, since word came that Ephraim's father was gravely wounded in battle a week past.

"Just rest, mother," Ephraim said. "I'll get your special tea, to help you sleep."

"I want to see him," she said, but already he could see that she was fading. "I need to see him…"

Once she was settled in and sleeping soundly, Ephraim stepped back outside. Elias and Egrel stood less than fifty paces from the cottage, and they both went silent upon seeing Ephraim.

"Brothers," he said, watching their stiff posture. Guilty, almost. "What is to happen to father's body?"

"The warriors are already building the funeral pyre," Egrel said, jerking his head toward the valley.

It was true; Ephraim moved closer to watch his father's brethren stacking lumber, wide and high.

"Will there be a ceremony?" Ephraim wondered. Usually death was a private affair, mourning kept to each individual family, but his father was no ordinary villager.

"No doubt." Elias shifted his stance, his eyes downcast.

"Mother will want to go," Ephraim said, sadness welling in his chest.

"She is too ill," Egrel shot back immediately, hostile. "I won't have you dragging her down to the village, making her health worse, just to keep her favor."

Ephraim's mouth opened and closed. Egrel had a cruel mind, always assuming the worst of everyone. What was there to say to that, really?

"She is sleeping now," Ephraim said, looking away instead.

"Let us go down, then." Elias, never one for two words when one would do. Head of the family now, it seemed.

Ephraim nodded and followed them, heart heavy.

As they trudged back up the hill from the ceremony, the pyre's ash and smoke still clinging to their clothes and hair, Egrel was the first to break the heavy silence.

"I've asked a sorcerer from a distant village to come and see to mother," he said, trading a heavy glance with Elias. "He should be here today."

"A sorcerer? Their services are very expensive. How will we pay for that?" Ephraim asked, frowning. "Our flocks are thinnest this time of year. We can hardly afford to give away as many sheep as he would surely ask."

"We will make an arrangement," Egrel said with a shrug. "Mother's health is most important, as I am sure you will agree."

Elias merely grunted, his expression dark as a thundercloud. There was something they weren't saying, Ephraim was sure of it. But what?

When they reached the cottage, the sorcerer was waiting for them. Swathed in many layers of woolen coats, hood shoved back to reveal a shock of perfectly white hair decades too old for his youthful face, he watched them all with darkly shining eyes.

"I am Egrel," Ephraim's brother said by way of introduction. "This is the older, Elias. And the youngest, Ephraim."

"I am Crane," the sorcerer said, inclining his head. "I haven't much time, so let us begin."

Ephraim and Egrel hovered as the man examined their mother, pushing back her thinning blonde hair, looking in her ears, pressing his finger against her parched tongue. It went on like that for some time, the man looking at her wrists and ankles, asking a few questions about whether she'd had fever, whether she'd met any strangers of late.

The sorcerer lay her in the bed and drew the covers over her once more.

"It is a malady of spirit, the most difficult to cure," he announced. He shot Egrel a meaningful glance. "I can mix something to heal her, but the ingredients are very, very rare."

"Do it," Egrel said without hesitation.

Ephraim wanted to ask outright what the cost would be, what understanding Egrel and Crane and Elias had between them, but he was afraid. Afraid that Crane might not cure his mother, afraid that the price they'd agreed to would be dark and shocking. After all, there was no way to un-know something once it'd been said aloud.

The man sat down at the broad kitchen table, clearing

away Mother's other medicines and herbs, and began to unpack various small jars and bottles from somewhere in his many cloaks. He pulled out a mortar and pestle and ground up a number of ingredients together, eventually producing a small amount of greenish, herbal liquid and pouring it into a glass vial.

"Give this with her tea, three times a day until it is gone. Do not miss a dose," the sorcerer said, handing it over to Egrel. He gathered his things, vanishing them all back into his cloaks, and stood.

Those dark eyes landed on Ephraim again, giving him a chill. Crane arched a brow, glancing at Egrel.

"I will take my payment now," he said simply.

A sense of foreboding slithered down Ephraim's spine a split second before Elias and Egrel sprung forward and grasped each of his arms, pulling them tight behind his body and cinching his wrists tight with a rough piece of cord.

"What—?!" was all Ephraim managed before Egrel clapped a pungent-smelling wad of cloth against his nose and mouth. Ephraim gagged at the oily residue that covered the cloth, but his muffled protest only made him drag in deep breaths of the heady odor.

His eyelids drooped, then his body, then he knew nothing.

The first thing Ephraim knew when he opened his eyes was that he was far, far away from home. The world shifted and rolled under him with merciless rhythm. There was a loud sound, rushing and hissing in time with the movement of the dark, cramped space where he lay.

A ship, he realized. He was in the underbelly of a ship, bound for parts unknown.

The next reality that sunk in was the feel of cool metal, wrapped around his neck and wrists. He couldn't make out the slave's collar and cuffs, they seemed to be invisible. But they were heavy and tight against his skin, all too real to him.

Once he worked up the nerve to explore his shadowy berth, he found a chamberpot, a flagon of stale water, and a box of mealy hard-tack biscuits. He couldn't even look at the food or water for a full day, his body falling victim to violent sickness caused by the movement of the ship. He'd never even seen the ocean, having in fact never been outside his village, but already he knew that he hated the sea.

Though he waited, no one came.

The ship rocked and rolled, and slowly he grew used to the feeling of it, his body adjusting.

He rationed his water and food.

Still, no one came.

At last, one day the ship's indomitable rhythm changed. The waves were harder, choppier... and then the movement ceased altogether. A door flung open and sunlight poured into the ship's hold; Ephraim's relief and terror were equal in measure.

An unfamiliar man with dark olive skin beckoned, speaking to Ephraim in a harsh and foreign tongue. Unsure what else to do, knowing he had nowhere to run in a strange land, Ephraim allowed himself to be pulled off the ship and loaded onto a cart piled high with boxes and bags. As if it wasn't clear enough that he was a possession, a piece of cargo...

Fingering the invisible metal of his collar, Ephraim swallowed. His eyes were wide, taking in the bustling docks and the towering white walls of a great city. The cart carried him straight through those gleaming walls, passing a hundred kinds of things: horses, people, cottages, stalls where people sold food and potions and swords and endless other items.

A city, Ephraim thought. *This must be a city.*

At the far end of Ephraim's sight line, a white marble palace rose against the endless blue sky. The cart stopped far from that, before a dark wood house several stories high, neat and tall. A prominent sign adorned the front, written in a language Ephraim had never seen, but there was an outlined sketch of a seductive, beckoning woman.

Why would Ephraim be brought to such a place?

The olive-skinned man yanked him off the cart and gave him a shove toward the front door. Ephraim went, feeling more helpless now than he had in the darkness of the ship's belly. When he stepped inside, a cloud of sweet, thick smoke greeted him. It was dark enough that he had to squint to make out the hazy shapes. The room was all polished wood and low furniture, cushions on the floor and soft-looking fabric draped over the windows.

Ephraim's captor propelled him though the room, down a dimly lit back hallway. At the very end, the man wrenched open a doorway and shoved Ephraim inside a simply furnished white room, pointing at a low, finely made white bed.

Ephraim took a seat as the door closed, leaving him alone. More waiting; it seemed that most of what he'd come to think of as his new life was waiting, waiting. There was nothing to look at or examine, not even a window in the whole room.

At length, the sorcerer himself stepped into the room.

"There you are," Crane said, as if Ephraim had somehow been late, as if he controlled any aspect of his current circumstances. At least Crane spoke Ephraim's language, a small comfort.

"Where are we?" Ephraim asked, his voice breaking a little from such a long period of disuse.

"That age, are we?" Crane said, chuckling. "The perfect age to be in your shoes, young man. To answer your question, you are in London."

"London," Ephraim repeated. "Where is that?"

Crane laughed.

"Only a world away from where I found you."

"Why am I here? Why would you want to take me from my family?" All the questions he'd turned over and over in his mind these last months tumbled out of his mouth unbidden.

"You won't agree with me now, but I think I saved you from a worse fate," Crane said, crossing his arms.

"Worse than wearing a collar?" Ephraim snapped.

To his surprise, Crane's lips curled up in amusement.

"I believe so, yes. I think you would have met with an unfortunate fate had I not taken you in the bargain. Your brother... Egrel, was it not? He offered you up quite eagerly. And the other one didn't stop him."

"You're lying," Ephraim hissed. "They would never do that."

"You were there," Crane said, his amusement fading. "And do not call me a liar again. You will regret it deeply."

"So I am a slave now, is that it? Why would you want me as a slave?" Ephraim challenged, though he'd had plenty of time to imagine a thousand vile reasons.

"You are much more than that. You are a djinn," Crane said, pronouncing it like *jen*.

"A genie in a lamp?" Ephraim scoffed, knowing the children's story well enough. "I am no such thing. I am a shape shifter, like my father."

"You are that, yes. But now you are more. You will see," Crane said. He produced a thin circle of shining, hammered gold. On the ring were three long, elegant gold keys. "Kneel."

Ephraim tried to open his mouth to argue, but fiery pain flashed through his entire body. Crane's command thundered through his mind, hammering at his very thoughts until he found himself on his knees, looking up at the sorcerer.

"What did you do?" Ephraim whispered.

"I wished for you to kneel. I spoke it aloud, holding the keys," he said, jiggling the keys in the air. "You had no choice. You live to serve now."

"Serve you? Why would you want that?" Ephraim asked. He scrambled back to his feet, heart pounding. His collar felt tighter than ever, and he pulled at it with clumsy, desperate fingers.

"You'll never get that off," Crane told him levelly. "You will serve whomever I give you to, for a time. And then the next… and then the next. That is how it shall be."

"There is no way to be free of it, ever?" Ephraim whimpered.

"Only if your master, the one holding the keys, gives up their greatest wish in order to free you. And don't think you can beg and borrow your way into it; it has to be of their own volition, for you can never ask to be freed." Crane tilted his head. "The power of the djinn, balanced with their eternal servitude. It is a balance you will come to know soon enough."

A knock on the door sounded, and Crane called over his shoulder for them to enter.

The door swung open to admit a tall, thin woman. All sharp angles and burning brown eyes, she couldn't have been a day below sixty-five years old… and none of her carefully applied powder or rouge hid a bit of it. She gave Ephraim a long, slow smile filled with unnaturally sharp, perfectly white teeth.

"Ah, Bethesda," Crane said. "As you requested, I have brought young Ephraim here to your house for his training. I want him treated very, very gently. He's very soft yet, and there will be many takers after your clientele have lost interest. You understand?"

Crane dangled the keys before her in the air.

"Yes," she snarled, snatching them from Crane with a scowl. Then she turned that sickening smile on Ephraim again. "You're prettier than I expected. Have you ever met a Vampyre, darling?"

"D-don't touch me!" Ephraim took an instinctive step

backward, which turned Bethesda's expression dark as night.

She jingled the keys in just the way Crane had, mocking.

"Sit on the bed." Those two words had his feet moving, had him stepping back and back until the bed bumped the backs of his thighs. He slowly sank down to sit. If he tried to resist, tried to turn away, every single nerve burned like wildfire. Bethesda grinned again, baring her teeth. "It won't be that bad. Well, not after the first time."

Bethesda reached out and slid her fingers into Ephraim's long hair, gripping it tight and tugging his head to the side. Exposing his neck, he realized. Bethesda's lips parted. As her mouth descended toward his neck, Ephraim knew the first true moment of despair in his young life.

CHAPTER 1

"So then he messaged me and was all like Netflix and Chill, and I was like, nooooo way Jose."

Dawn smacked her gum, flipping her dark hair over her shoulder. Sophie examined her friend and coworker for a moment, admiring her smooth cocoa skin and impeccable dress. Dawn was always done up to the nines, makeup and nails and hair perfectly matching the outfit of the day.

Sophie looked down at her own thrice-worn jeans and wrinkled ivory silk top and sighed. Dawn always outclassed Sophie in the having-her-shit-together department, but today Sophie was practically slumming it. She hadn't been out in the sun since midsummer, so she'd completely lost her tan. Her long blonde hair was a wild mess of unbridled waves, and her nails... well, it was better not to get into the finer points. It wasn't pretty.

"So then he had the nerve to say I was a tease!" Dawn said, pulling a face.

"Mmmhm," Sophie said. She scrunched up her face

and stared at the rain hitting the broad plate glass window that faced Royal Street, one of New Orleans's most popular high-end shopping districts. The weather had killed all the walk-in traffic to Sophie's little dressmaker's shop, and Sophie knew she should be doing any number of little tasks. She and her sales assistant, Dawn, should be dusting the place from top to bottom, doing inventory, rotating out some of the stock, or at least changing the elegant mannequins in the front window.

Sophie glanced at the mannequins for the briefest moment, then looked away. She knew well enough what they looked like; all done up in pastel silk dresses, trimmed out in full 1950s flair. It was a beautiful display, though it was over two months old at this point. Tears stung her eyes every single time she thought about the stupid dolls for more than half a second.

Lily picked those outfits. She stood there and dressed those mannequins, touched them. She smiled and laughed and frowned while she was setting up their display.

And then,

It was her last display, on her last day of her whole life. It was the last thing she touched before...

Thus the tears.

"Sophie!"

Sophie turned to look at Dawn, guiltily wiping at the corners of her eyes.

"Oh, girl..." Dawn said, hopping up from her perch behind the cash register and walking around to hug Sophie. "We have to get you a hobby or something, honey. I love you, I really do, but you are spending all your time focusing on what happened to your sister and no time on what's happening to *you*, right here and now."

"I know," Sophie said, shaking her head. "I get up in the morning and I think I have a handle on it, but by lunch I'm just…"

"It's okay," Dawn said, giving her another little hug. "I was thinking maybe we could go to that Wiccan power circle thing tonight, since you said you haven't been able to do any magic since… Lately, I mean."

"I don't know," Sophie said, rubbing her hands over her face, trying to wake herself up a little bit. She was exhausted all the time, but she never really slept. Hell, she never did much of anything… it seemed like food, sleep, and basic self-care only happened when they were absolutely necessary. "I don't feel much of a spark. Besides, I was never more than a low level white witch. It's not like I'm going to get powerful all the sudden. I don't think that's how it works."

Dawn blew out a breath. Sophie could see that her friend was frustrated, holding back something she wanted to say, but afraid to hurt Sophie's feelings. It was very, very easy to hurt Sophie's feelings these days, ever since…

"Lily died," Dawn blurted out. "Your baby sister died. And it was terrible, like the worst thing you'll ever go through in your whole life. A little piece of you went away, and it is never going to come back. I get that, I swear I do." Dawn took a deep breath. "But the rest of you is withering away. This stuff, keeping the mannequins the same, refusing to scatter her ashes, that thing you do where you just go and sit outside Bellocq and *watch*…"

Sophie's mouth dropped open.

"You know about that?!" She squeaked, her face going red. So maybe she liked to go to the Vampyre club where Lily had spent her last few hours alive. Well, less *go to* and more *sit outside and brood*, waiting for... something.

A clue. A single idea of what could possibly have happened to her innocent, kind, open-hearted eighteen year old sister. The one person who'd always been there, the only family Sophie ever had.

Had. Past tense.

"Hey!" Dawn said, snapping her fingers. "This right here? The weird zoning out? This is what I am talking ab0ut, to a T."

"Sorry," Sophie apologized again.

"Don't... don't be sorry, Soph. You just... you can't go on like this. You need to go on a vacation, or re-engage with the Wiccan coven, or... hell, I don't know. Start sky diving. Anything! You need to get mad, or get energized, or get something. Anything is better than just being sad every hour of the day."

Sophie didn't respond, just rubbed her face again and stretched.

"I should go get some coffee," she said, trying to change the subject.

"Uh-uh," Dawn said, crossing her arms. "You are going to go home and try to sleep. If you need it, I will call someone and buy you some pot."

"Ugh, no," Sophie said, but Dawn wasn't interested in her protests.

"Fine! Get drunk, go for a run, whatever. Get tired, get some rest. And don't you dare think of coming into the shop for the rest of the week. I will call Lacey and Maryanne and we will cover all your shifts."

"Oh, Dawn, I couldn't," Sophie said, rolling her eyes.

Dawn reached out and grabbed Sophie's hand, giving it a squeeze.

"I love you. I really, really do. But if you show up here for the rest of the week, I quit. And I know the rest of the staff will follow me. The store is a mess. Let me take over for the week, and when you come back it will be…" she paused thoughtfully. "Maybe not perfect, but better. And more importantly, different."

She twirled a finger to indicate the merchandise racks that had slowly begun to accumulate dust. Sophie knew that Dawn couldn't wait to change the mannequins, and it made her heart give a lurch. Still, this wasn't a fight Sophie was interested in having. Dawn was her closest friend, and sometimes it was better just to take her advice.

Besides, there was something she needed to do tonight…

And it wasn't catching up on her sleep.

"You sure you want to do this, white witch?"

The woman's Haitian accent was a little slap in the face, a startling bit of reality. Her dark skin gleamed in the light of the small fire that lay between them, her teeth flashing white against the darkness of the sultry night air. She held her closed fist out over the fire, palm down, awaiting Sophie's decision.

Could this really be happening?

You're not hallucinating this. You're not dreaming. You are actually in the underbelly of the Gray Market, paying a Vodun priestess to do spells that require dark magic.

Blood magic, actually. Just the thought of such dark magic sent icy fingers of fear creeping down her spine. She and Lily were raised Wiccan, so Sophie had no excuse. She knew better than to come near something like *this* with a ten foot pole.

Sophie, you really have done it this time, Lily would have said.

"Yes," came out of Sophie's mouth, a second before the thought even formed in her mind. She was all instinct and angry hurt right now, no room for second thoughts and self-recrimination.

The priestess arched a brow and shrugged, then dropped a little bundle of hair wrapped around a tiny glass vial into the fire. It hissed and cracked for a minute, the smell of burning hair made Sophie cough. The priestess merely stared into the fire, which abruptly flared and changed color.

"Ah," the priestess sighed. "Your sister is gone, as you believed."

"I knew that already. I felt her pass from the world," Sophie said, though she'd already explained that much.

"Patience," the woman cautioned, raising a finger in warning. "There is more. Your sister was taken by a very, very dangerous creature. He is a Loa, a greater spirit of the Voodoo and Vodun, taken to flesh to walk in this world."

"What's his name? What did he do to Lily?" Suddenly

Sophie's throat was tight, her whole body coiled and ready to fight.

"I cannot say his name, lest I might summon him," the priestess said, shaking her head. "He took your sister, used her body as a vessel to allow him into the human world. Your sister was a virgin, was she not?"

"Y-yes," Sophie whispered, her mouth going dry. That was Lily's big secret, something no one else knew about her. Sophie's sister had been saving herself for marriage, though she was too shy to talk about it.

The priestess knowing that fact about Lily... it made all of this seem real, very suddenly. It was a shock to her system, knowing that Lily was... on the other side?

"She's in heaven now?" Sophie asked, her cheeks flushing. She wasn't Christian, exactly, having come up as a pagan, but that was the only way she could think to phrase her question.

The answer was not what she'd hoped. The priestess gave a slow shake of her head, looking sympathetic.

"No, I'm afraid not, my dear. She is... in between."

Sophie narrowed her gaze.

"You are talking about my dead sister. Please tell me you aren't going to try to sell me some charm or spell to help her move on," she accused.

The woman's expression went stony.

"You already paid me for this," she said, waving her hand around the fire. "I am no thief. Your sister is in between worlds because a piece of her still rides with the Loa, though he has long since shed her body. One as powerful as him, he must take a new Vessel every few days, I imagine. Maybe more."

Sophie felt like her heart had been ripped from her chest.

"Did she suffer?" she found herself asking.

The priestess didn't answer, which was answer enough.

"I believe... I believe a little part of her may still exist, along with the Loa. Like, how can you say, he is riding horseback and she sits behind him?" The woman gestured with her fingers, to indicate two people sitting close together. "She rides with him, all the Vessels ride along with him, forever."

Sophie turned that over in her mind for a minute.

"If there is a piece of her that is still alive, we could bring her back."

"We?" The priestess's eyebrows shot up. "Not I."

"I meant to say, someone. Someone *could* do that."

"You do not want that, white witch. You would not get back the same person you knew and loved, I assure you."

"But it is possible?"

The priestess thought it over for a moment, and then shook her head.

"Not in the way you mean, no. And the body is gone... There is nothing left to bring back, I am sure." She hesitated.

"Tell me," Sophie urged. "Anything, anything at all."

"If it were me, and I cared very much about this person, I would want to free their spirit. Allow them to move on to the next world."

"I do, I do want that. How can I do that?"

The woman pursed her lips, thinking.

"There is a way, I think. If you were to destroy the Loa,

that might work. If you pulled him out of the human world, yanked him back into the spirit world by the roots. Then destroy him…" She took a deep breath. "You would need a way to kill a Loa, though. Very rare."

"Could you find such a thing?" Sophie asked, excitement stirring in the pit of her stomach.

Another considering glance.

"The magic you would need to do this thing, it would be so dark… You would never be a white witch again. You understand?"

"Fine. Anything," Sophie insisted.

"If the Loa does not kill you first, the stain on your soul will. You may not… you may not enter the same afterlife as your sister, white witch. Would it be worth that to free her?"

Sophie didn't even hesitate.

"Of course."

"Fine," the priestess said. She pulled out a piece of paper and scrawled something on it, handing it over the fire to Sophie. "Wait until you hear from me again, white witch. Do not approach the Loa without the object I will bring you. To do so would be to assure your failure."

Sophie opened her mouth to respond, but the priestess picked up a bucket of black ash and banked the fire without notice, vanishing into the darkness leaving Sophie alone in the quiet night air. Sophie stumbled back down the rambling back alleys of the Gray Market she'd followed to find the priestess in the first place, emerging near the front doors of Sloane General.

Once she was back in the Gray Market's hazy street

lights, she unfolded the piece of paper the priestess had pressed on her.

It had but two words: Papa Aguiel.

Closing her eyes, she knew the first moment of elation she'd felt since the moment she'd woken in her bed, knowing instantly that her little sister was no longer in the world.

Vengeance was so, so close... and she would have it.

Sophie stood across from the rambling residence the Alpha Guardians referred to as the Manor, biding her time. She'd stood here for four nights already, gone so far as to break some of the house's minor wards. All because she was following a tip from a Gray Market acquaintance who said that the Guardians were pursuing the same quarry as she.

Papa Aguiel.

The name rang through her head, over and over until she thought her heart might beat to the rhythm of his name, until her veins ran thick with the sound of it. *Pa-pa A-gu-iel, Pa-pa A-gu-iel,* her heart seemed to say.

A flurry of activity drew her attention to the front steps of the Manor. Several people stepped outside, and Sophie raised her binoculars. There, on the ground. A dark haired man in a long black coat, utterly collapsed.

How had she missed this, the one person her contact had told her to watch for?

Ephraim Crane. Soon-to-be Alpha Guardian. Immortal.

And most importantly, genuine article djinn. Those weren't exactly floating around freely these days, so she needed to focus.

She could not screw this up. It was her only chance to save Lily.

Free Lily, not save her. She cannot be saved, a quiet voice in the back of her head protested, but Sophie shoved it deep down.

She'd worked so hard for this moment. She'd handed the keys to her store over to Dawn, suddenly and without explanation. She never planned to return, though Dawn didn't know that.

She'd closed up her house, given Dawn a big draught of cash to take care of the tabby they kept in the shop and any other incidentals. Claiming she was going on a long-term cruise, Sophie had simply... slipped away from her old life.

And now she was here, on the cusp of everything she wanted. So, so close.

The group at the Manor's front door managed to get Ephraim to his feet. Sophie had seen but a single photo of him, nearly as blurry as his face was now from such a distance, but it was enough to know that he was handsome. Something else, too, in his expression. She couldn't put her finger on it.

Not that it mattered...

Sophie realized that her mind was drifting, and wondered when the last time she'd slept was. Not in days, at least. She was burning her magic at both ends, all in pursuit of this...

Dropping her binoculars, she reached in her left

pocket and pulled out the object that had taken her over a month to procure. A beautiful set of three keys on a ring, all made of the most finely wrought gold Sophie had ever laid eyes on. The gold seemed to warm to her touch, almost comforting, glowing softly from within somehow.

She turned over her left hand, palm up, and saw the light gray lines of enchanted ink that lay there in delicate swirls. The only tattoo she had, the one she'd shared with Lily. An early birthday present on her sister's eighteenth birthday.

never lost, it read in feminine script.

always found, Lily's had said.

If only that were remotely true, if only the giddy dreams they'd shared had been more than a foolish fantasy…

Closing her fingers tight around the keys, she tried not to remember just the way it felt when her tattoo pulsed that night, the night Lily died. The thick, dark lines of ink faded to the softest gray, just as Lily faded from the human realm. A distress signal, from beyond the Veil…

Taking a deep breath, she steadied herself and resisted the urge to rub her fingers over the tattoo. If Lily could feel her now, somehow, Sophie was dead sure her sister wouldn't approve.

But Lily wasn't here. Lily was dead, and Sophie would have her vengeance if it was the last thing she ever did, if it stole away her very last breath.

"You're going to have to be a lot more beguiling than this," she told herself aloud.

If she was ever going to cozy up to the djinn and gain access to the places only he could take her, she would need to at least pretend not to be dead inside. She tried for a smile, and though she couldn't see it, she knew it was gruesome.

No matter. She had time to practice. She'd do anything she needed to do to carry out the rest of her mission.

Tomorrow, she thought. *Tomorrow, it begins.*

Tucking the keys in her pocket, she turned and sauntered back into the moonless New Orleans night.

CHAPTER 2

*E*phraim paced the floor in the rooms he'd been assigned in the Manor, unable to rest. After a day's sleep and a long state-of-affairs meeting with the Guardians, he learned about Papa Aguiel and what Mere Marie believed to be the coming war to save the city and possibly all of mankind. Now, though, his thoughts returned to his new master.

Sophie.

The moment that his ownership transferred from one person to another, Ephraim always became aware of his new master. He got a few glimpses of the person, usually, just enough to get a sense of them and what they looked like. A cosmic heads up to let him know what to look for, what to expect.

He'd felt the pull thousands of times. At worse, the knowledge provoked a sort of teeth-grinding anxiety in him, knowing he needed to fulfill a fresh set of hopes and dreams. At best, a dull sort boredom, a sense of having served that *sort* of person before.

This time felt different, though he couldn't say why. Sophie was beautiful, with long blonde hair, a heart-shaped face set with full pink lips, and a curvy-yet-petite figure that Ephraim found appealing.

That in itself wasn't remarkable, though. Ephraim had served hundreds of beautiful people, women and men alike, and he knew that one's looks were no indicator of what lay beneath. He'd learned that lesson early on in his life, and had been reminded time and again.

No, this was something... else. He felt foreboding, but not in the way that he'd felt with some of his crueler masters. Like the Grecian brothel owner who'd pimped him out to leagues of customers, anyone with enough coin and an eye for tall, dark, and handsome men with Ephraim's coloring. Silky chin-length chestnut hair, light olive skin, bright yellow-green eyes. He was big and broad, having grown into the spitting image of his father's muscular warrior's build.

His lips thinned at the thought of the whip-thin, pale, balding brothel owner. One of the darkest souls he'd encountered in all his days.

None was worse than the assassin, though. Ephraim had been given over to a shadowy slave owner who bought and trained 'assets', as he called them, with a sole purpose. Murder, quick and violent yet subtle.

How many had Ephraim killed for the man? Hundreds? A thousand?

With the assassin feeding him tincture of poppy, what would later be known as opium, Ephraim had slid into that role all too easily. Standing in the Manor's spacious living room, Ephraim looked down at his hands, marveling that he'd ever got all the blood and viscera off them, that he'd ever made them clean again.

He balled his hands into fists, his mind circling back around to his current obsession.

Sophie, Sophie. Where are you?

He'd sought her for some days, running himself ragged. Before he found himself on the Guardians' doorstep, he'd fought his way through a Kriiluuth demon's lair, on the word that Sophie had been there.

No luck, but it did make him wonder what kind of trouble his new master might be in. The Kriiluuth's lair was in the darkest, farthest reaches of the Gray Market's labyrinthine world. The couple of flashes he'd gotten of her, she was laughing with friends, dancing and having fun at a second line, working diligently folding and organizing things in a store where she likely worked. She wore brightly colored, stylish dresses, and she was perfectly groomed and manicured.

That person seemed light-hearted and good. Kind, even. Not like she had some bottomless void inside her, which was the main quality of people who came to possess Ephraim's keys. No one came across a djinn by accident; it was either through fate or a lot of hard work, and inevitably the person *needed* him. Needed things from him. Dark and dangerous things.

So what was she doing skulking in shadowy corners of the Gray Market?

Ephraim's lips twisted. Maybe this was all just wishful thinking. None of the others who'd owned him had been anything but selfish, focused on their own needs and nothing else. Why should Sophie be any different?

Ephraim would do anything she asked. *Had* to do it. *Needed* to do it. If she said jump off a bridge, he'd do it. Kill a puppy? He'd do it, when the pain grew bad enough. Accomplish a task so Herculean and impossible that just considering it would devastate a normal man? Done. Somehow, some way.

That was the seductive power of Ephraim's gift. No one had ever been able to resist, not in a thousand years.

She wouldn't sacrifice her greatest desire just to free Ephraim, no matter how kind she might be. Who in their right mind would do that, in the face of what Ephraim's powers could give them? Why did he feel even the slightest flicker of hope?

Ephraim went still, the thought slipping away like a few grains of sand in his open fingers.

Sophie. He could *feel* her. She was close, waiting for him.

He let the sensation of her presence pull him forward into the Manor's foyer and outside. His mouth fell open when he saw her standing on the curb, only a hundred yards away. Gone was the cultured, well-dressed, smiling woman he'd seen in his visions.

This woman was dressed head to toe in black leather and denim, her blonde hair pulled back in a severe ponytail. She was still beautiful, there was absolutely no denying it, but there was also something about her that screamed *woman on a mission*.

At first, he thought that her beauty was just magnetic, that he found her so alluring. But then, some little part of Ephraim, shoved deep down inside… some resolute, indisputable sense of self rose, and it was certain of one thing.

Mate.

He took a step toward Sophie, and she moved toward him at the same time. Her chin lifted, and for a moment he thought he saw the same expression on her face, thought he saw her pupils dilate and contract, making her clear blue eyes brighten and darken quick as a heart's beat.

She feels it too, he thought.

Then she lifted her hand, a glint of gold drawing his gaze. Ephraim's moment of dazzling, blinding hope flared and then died when he saw what she held up for him to see.

His keys.

He had to give himself a sharp shake to stop the painful squeeze in his chest.

What did you expect? He reprimanded himself. *This is what happens when you're stupid enough to hope. You know better.*

Moving closer, he noticed that Sohpie's clothes weren't the only dark thing about her. Her aura lit up for just a moment, tranquil lavender and pink and white close to her heart. Further out, though, it darkened. Around the edges it went from royal purple to midnight blue to black, like a piece of paper with singed edges.

She was in transition, her aura slowly darkening as she tainted the inner wellspring of her power, no doubt with some very dark magic. Another mystery, a piece of the puzzle that matched perfectly with her stalking demons in the Gray Market.

Suddenly, she was only steps away from him, looking him up and down.

"What's your name, djinn?" she asked, gaze narrowed. Expecting a fight.

"Ephraim," he said, letting his head drop a few inches. She was gorgeous and tempting, and he wanted nothing more than to move closer. Touch her, taste her.

Mate, rang through his head now, over and over. *Mate. Mate. Mate.*

After she'd presented the keys, though, his desire for her made him feel... dirty. Weak. He kept his gaze low, unwilling to share all the emotions that were no doubt flitting through his eyes. He'd never been one to conceal his emotions, especially since none of his masters ever cared how he felt.

Now, though... he wouldn't give that part of himself to her, not if he could help it.

"You're the only one that can help me, Ephraim," she said, a softly melodic quality to her voice.

His lips curled up in a humorless smile.

"Not the first time I've heard those words," he said, canting his head. "I suppose you should come inside, the Guardians have been waiting."

He didn't miss the surprise in her expression, but he turned his back and marched inside before he could read further into it. Learning more about her, feeding the curiosity about her that filled him inside, it would only lead to the deepest kind of disappointment.

Mere Marie awaited them inside, seated on an overstuffed love seat, her voluminous white robes arranged around her like a cloud.

"This is Sophie?" Mere Marie asked, a cynical brow arching. Her eyes moved over Sophie, no doubt reading her tarnished aura just as Ephraim had a few moments ago.

"This is Sophie," Sophie said, her brows pulling together as she frowned. "You must be Marie La—"

"Mere Marie," said Rhys, the big redheaded Scot who served as head Guardian. "I'm Rhys. Let me make introductions."

He went around and introduced five of the Guardians and their respective mates, explaining that one of the Guardians had a new baby and wouldn't be involved in the planning stages. A pair of identical Fae, new to Ephraim's eyes, were introduced as the Guardians' most recent additions.

"I'm Kieran, this is Kellan. Our mate is at work," one of them explained in a thick Irish brogue. He rolled his eyes. "She says she's less interested in the coming apocalypse and more interested in *helping people*."

"She's a doctor," the other one cut in, elbowing his brother. "We're astoundingly proud of our Sera."

"Right," Mere Marie said once all the chit chat was done. "You've come at just the right time, the planning stages."

"The planning stages of what, exactly?" Sophie asked, crossing her arms. Her gaze wandered around the room, taking everything in. Ephraim could tell that she was shrewd, certainly intelligent. The dark circles under her eyes and the tension in her shoulders spoke of a bone-deep exhaustion; clearly, lovely Sophie wasn't just dabbling in dark magic, she was on the run from something.

"Of taking down Papa Aguiel," Mere Marie said, mirroring Sophie's stance by crossing her arms and squaring her jaw. "That's why you're here, isn't it?"

Sophie looked surprised again, but quickly covered it with a simple nod.

"That's why I'm here," she affirmed.

Mere Marie and Sophie spent a few minutes chatting, if you could call it that. It was closer to thinly veiled accusations and barbs, but Ephraim just stayed out of it. His ultimate allegiance was to whoever held his keys, not to the Guardians. It was useless to take sides in an argument when anything he said might come back to hurt him later.

Instead of participating, he merely studied her, tried to understand the connection he felt to her. His bear perked up, interested in Sophie, cautiously calling for Ephraim to get closer, closer.

If only, he lamented. No, this must be some kind of cruel joke. He'd always hoped to find a mate, the way his father found his mother. Instant, consuming, destined. But he'd imagined that it would happen once he'd managed to free himself.

He hadn't even fantasized about being free in nearly a century, and his desire to find a mate died long before that. Ephraim squinted into the distance, trying to pinpoint the moment when he'd given up on having a family and a mate of his own, but he couldn't begin to guess.

The brothel in Greece, probably. Stretched out on a rack,

blindfolded and bound, being ridden hard by a masochistic woman three time his age while she raked her nails up and down his body and screamed at him to make her come... Yeah, somewhere around that point, if he had to guess.

When the meeting broke up suddenly, Ephraim realized he'd ogled her for almost ten minutes without hearing a word that was said, much less participating. Rhys clapped Ephraim on the shoulder, giving him a knowing sort of look.

"It's hard on everyone," he said quietly.

"What is?" Ephraim asked, gently shrugging off the other Guardian's touch.

"Meeting your fated mate. None of us has had an easy go of it," Rhys confided in him.

Ephraim went rigid. How could the other man possibly know about the pull Ephraim felt?

"Your pheromones are going wild," Rhys said, arching a brow. "Both of you."

"Ephraim?" Sophie called.

Ephraim didn't reply to Rhys, turning away in favor of attending to Sophie. Lesser of two evils, in this case.

"Can we go somewhere... quieter?" she asked, her brow furrowing. Her cheeks heated, though Ephraim couldn't imagine why. He glanced around and shrugged.

"Outside?" he suggested.

The quick flash of disappointment in her eyes could have been his imagination, but he didn't think so.

"Fine," she said, leading the way out a set of French doors and into the back yard.

When they stood in the moonlight, alone and out of

sight of the others, she crossed her arms and gave him a measured glance.

"So what is this?" She asked, pursing her lips.

"What is what?" Ephraim asked, struggling to keep from adding the word *mistress* to the end. Ephraim might be a dominant, world-weary asshole, but some part of him desperately wanted to please this woman. The weakness of it made him sick to his stomach, but he just forced it down.

"*This*, this," she said, gesturing to each of them in turn. "The… draw. Don't you feel it?"

Ephraim nodded, but didn't dare add anything more.

"Well?" Sophie asked, her voice hard. After a moment, she softened a little. "You don't feel it, do you?"

Ephraim huffed a sigh and shoved his fingers through his thick, dark hair.

"Of course I do," he snapped.

Her brows raised in a delicate arch.

"If you know what it means, I want you to tell me," she said.

His eyes dropped to her hands, checking to see if she had the keys ready and waiting.

"Is that a command?" He asked.

"Only if it has to be," she shot back.

His lips pulled back from his teeth, but he didn't resist the acidic words that burst free.

"Can't be. I thought we were—" he had to stop himself there, shaking his head.

"What? Tell me, Ephraim!" She insisted.

"I thought we were mates," he hissed. The word was sour on his tongue, an impossibility. Fate, his nemesis all these years, even she could not be so cruel. A destined love, a mate of his own... a master who owned him, who could control his every breath.

It was unthinkable. Ephraim couldn't look at her for another second, the ice in his chest beginning to crack and ache. He whirled and headed back inside, lest she give him another command.

CHAPTER 3

*P*lop.

Papa Aguiel scowled down at the blob of flesh that landed on the knee of his suit, clinging. He reached up to find that the patch of dark skin had liberated itself from near his left ear.

Shaking his head, he hefted the ceremonial dagger and pushed onward. He was changing Vessels at least once a day now, and his options for suitable virgins were running quite low.

No matter, he thought to himself, and it was true. His habit of changing bodies was at an end, because he'd finally secured the objects he needed to finish the ritual. The dagger, ripped from the dying hands of a Tibetan magic man who'd held it close for a Kith lifetime. A vial of dragon's blood, procured from one of the Alpha Guardians during a recent battle. And a jar of essence, the product of months of effort on Papa Aguiel's part, all his hopes and fears and family ties magically condensed into a simple glass mason jar.

He stalked through the dark New Orleans night, heaving a sigh of relief when he finally walked under the highway overpass. Above him, cars whirred and zoomed along I-10, but he paid no attention.

Looking around, he made sure the area was clear of pedestrians. No need for anyone to see the inner workings of his magic, just as a precaution. He found just the spot he needed, the place where all the Gates of Guinee aligned just so.

Not a particularly auspicious spot for the magic he was about to work, but again it did not matter. All that mattered was his task, which would stop the decomposition of his current Vessel and bring him into the final stage of his great plan.

Papa Aguiel gave himself a little shake, trying to rouse the energy level in his failing body. He took out the jar of essence, glancing at it one final time. Then he shrugged and unceremoniously smashed it on the ground before him, laying a snare for friendly and familial spirits that would power him through the last stage of his journey.

Next he dumped out the vial of dragon's blood, which smoked fiercely when it touched the essence. The ground rippled and heaved, looking for all the world like a living thing, and the Veil between the worlds shimmered faintly.

Papa Aguiel grinned as he half-lunged, half-fell forward, sinking the dagger deep into the Veil and swinging it upward. The Veil parted as easily as flesh beneath a scalpel, drawing back to reveal a darkly glowing portal.

Success.

Holding his hands up and letting his oh-so-heavy head

roll forward on his weak neck, he began his real work. Summoning the spirits who would strengthen and sustain him, that would give him utter dominion over the human realm.

Even the Guardians couldn't stop him now.

After a few moments, the first tentative tendril of spirit slid from the gash in the Veil, slipping into the world to swirl around Papa Aguiel's dying body.

He sucked in a deep breath, inhaling the spirit whole into his lungs. It fortified him, the first of many that would do so.

He grinned again, feeling his crumbling lips reforming on his face.

"It begins."

CHAPTER 4

I thought we were mates.

Sophie stayed in the back yard after Ephraim stormed off, the truth of his words ringing through her, bone-deep.

"Fuck!" she said, pressing her knuckles against her teeth.

This could not be happening. She couldn't have a mate, not right now... not *him*. Six months ago, she'd been actively searching for her life partner, daydreaming about mated life and wedding bells. She wanted a huge human-style wedding, in addition to a Wiccan ceremony and whatever her mate's traditions might be.

And Ephraim couldn't be more her type, his big finely-honed frame, straight dark hair, and bright yellow-green eyes lighting up every nerve ending in her entire body. Hell, six months ago Sophie would have walked right up to him and asked him to take her straight to bed.

But the Sophie of six months ago hadn't suffered the

losses present-Sophie had. And no amount of cheer could overcome the issues inherent in her present situation.

Such as: what happens when your mate is also your slave?

Sophie thought she might actually faint. She walked over to the high wood fence surrounding the Manor's back yard and sat down, leaning against it as she buried her face in her arms.

For the first time since she'd learned Papa Aguiel's name, the enormity of her task overwhelmed her, a sob breaking free from her throat.

What the hell had she ever done to deserve this? First Lily was ripped from her life, now she was given a mate she could never have? For once Sophie took what she wanted from him, she would be dead, or at least so corrupted by dark magic that she couldn't return to this realm and live in the light again.

She gulped in big gasps of air, trying to think rationally.

There was more than one kind of fate, wasn't there? Maybe he was fated to her in order to help her eliminate Papa Aguiel. Maybe Sophie wasn't meant to have a romantic mate. Instead, destiny had given her the man she needed most, bound him to her to make her mission easier.

After all, if Ephraim fell in love with her hard and fast the way the stories of fated mates said he should, he would do as she asked… no matter what she asked. Maybe he wouldn't even question her and would simply clear the way for her to achieve her goal.

Avenge her sister, save the world.

A cold laugh bubbled from her lips.

Is that all? She asked herself. *Just saving mankind, no big deal.*

Thrusting her hand into her pocket, she drew out the keys that ruled Ephraim's entire life. They warmed to her touch again, sending a chill down her spine.

What are you becoming? A little voice asked, but Sophie couldn't listen, wouldn't. She crammed them back in the pocket of her leather jacket, then got to her feet. All the while, ignoring that persistent whisper.

Wrong, wrong, wrong.

She shoved back her left sleeve and looked at her tattoo again, the lines so light they were nearly silver in the moonlight. She drew in a deep breath, centering herself.

A mate could wait, but Lily's very *soul* was in limbo. Not to mention that from all accounts Papa Aguiel was going to make the skies rain blood... and that was just for starters.

"You're doing the right thing," she whispered to herself, ignoring the stinging numbness in her lips. "You're doing the only thing you can."

With that, she wiped at her damp cheeks and straightened her hair, blowing out a breath when she realized she was primping. For *him*.

The one she'd just determined wasn't meant to be a romantic mate.

Damn, girl. Get your head on straight.

She steeled herself and headed back inside, finding that Ephraim hadn't gone far. He was standing in the kitchen, his expression dark and closed off, contemplating a mug of coffee.

"I need you to understand something," she said, skipping the niceties.

Ephraim favored her with a curious glance, but didn't speak. Emotions ran riot over his face, but without knowing him better Sophie couldn't begin to guess at some of them.

"I am going to take down Papa Aguiel. I don't care about anything else, and I won't stop until he's dead... or I am." She tossed the words down like a gauntlet, challenging Ephraim to say a word against her convictions.

He watched her for a moment, seeming to consider her words fully. Then, "Involving yourself with the Guardians, not to mention trying to take on a Loa of Papa Aguiel's power... It's more than a risk. It's a death wish."

An ugly smile lit Sophie's lips.

"I've heard that before," she said.

Another long pause from Ephraim.

"You know what I am, obviously," he said, cocking his head. "You could ask for anything. I would take you anywhere. If we are fated mates, as I think we both suspect... Are you not tempted to ask me to simply take you away from it all? It would be well within my power."

For the barest moment, Sophie's heart squeezed so tight she almost couldn't breathe. *Tempted* didn't begin to describe it.

"I can't," she uttered. "There's only one thing I'm fated for, and it's taking out Papa Aguiel. I don't have time or room for anything else in my life."

"Why you?" He asked, those gorgeous eyes scanning her face, seeking. "Something personal, I should think?"

Before she could answer, Rhys pounded into the room.

"The Veil has been breached," the Scot huffed, out of breath. "We are going to see the site. Ephraim, we'd like you to come. Just you, for now."

Rhys gave Sophie an apologetic shrug, then left.

"Wait—" Sophie tried to follow the Guardian as he vanished toward the back yard, but just ended up stumbling over her own feet. Exhaustion won out over coordination, and she nearly fell flat on her face.

Except that didn't happen. Instead, her descent was abruptly stopped by Ephraim's strong hands on her waist, pulling her close to his body as he supported her.

"I got you," he said, giving her ribs a gentle squeeze as she gripped his arms to regain her balance.

Suddenly Sophie was pressed up against him, staring right into those lovely eyes. Something dark and deadly lurked below the surface there, barely hidden. Something else too, though. Something...

Sophie licked her lips as her eyes dropped to his mouth, and it was everything she could do not to move closer and take in a lungful of his masculine scent.

"Why us?" She wondered aloud, meeting his gaze again.

Ephraim flinched, every inch of his formidable body going rigid, and released her like she was a burning coal in his bare hands. The distrust plain all over his face was no surprise, but it stung more than Sophie knew it ought to.

What did you expect? She chided herself as she watched Ephraim turn and follow Rhys's path out of the room.

She'd committed to a dark path. Now she was living that truth, and there was nothing for it but to keep moving.

CHAPTER 5

"Two days you've been gone!"

Ephraim sighed at the anger in Sophie's voice. The second he walked back into the Manor, still dripping with Vampyre blood from a particularly nasty fight in the Central Business District, Sophie stuck to him like glue.

"I know," Ephraim said, bowing his head. He shouldn't feel sorry, not at all. He was merely doing what he ought, working with the Guardians to protect people like Sophie against the quickly-growing chaos in the city. Still, she was his master. And in theory, his mate. It was hard to resist the urge to go to her, touch her, make sure she was okay.

She followed him up the stairs to the suite of rooms he'd been assigned, her cheeks flushed with anger.

"What could you possibly have been doing for two days straight?" She demanded to know. "I thought you were dead!"

Ephraim glanced at her as he toed off his heavy black combat boots.

"And? Why should you care?" He asked.

Sophie's eyes narrowed.

"That's unfair," she said, folding her arms across her chest.

"I don't think it is. You came into possession of some keys. That gives you a lot of sway over me, which I cannot control. Otherwise, you don't know me. We're strangers."

It felt like a lie coming out of his mouth, but it was the plain truth. Sophie was a beautiful stranger, no matter how connected he might feel to her. They'd barely even spoken, much less discovered anything deeper.

No, she was concerned about him as an investment in… whatever nefarious plans she'd laid. At the moment, Ephraim was simply too weary to care.

"I care whether you live or die," she said, looking annoyed. "And you can't just vanish for two days without a word!"

Ephraim stripped off his shirt, enjoying the way her eyes went wide as she checked out his body. The resulting flush of her cheeks was the most pleasurable thing Ephraim had experienced in a long, long time. She flipped back her long mane of blonde hair, which he noticed she'd left down, loose, curly, and tempting.

"You could have ordered me to come back," he told her, ripping his gaze away from where it had wandered, to her amazing tits and perfectly curved hips.

"I wouldn't have done that," she said, turning her face away.

"No?" He asked. "I don't see why not."

She bit her lip, letting his question hang in the air.

"I'm about to get naked," Ephraim told her frankly. "So unless you're going to join me in the shower, I suggest you wait in the library."

He pointed toward the door, and was rewarded with Sophie's blazing cheeks as she stormed from the room with a huff. Ephraim groaned at himself as he stripped down, at the fact that he'd run himself ragged the last few days and he was still already hard as a rock after talking to her for two seconds.

"Pathetic," he told himself as he walked into the bathroom.

As much as he wanted to stand under the shower's hot water forever, possibly even take his cock in his fist and release some seriously pent up lust, he kept it brief. In and out in a matter of minutes, because the truth was, he did feel a little guilty for disappearing for two days.

How fucked up was that? Two days, a passing attempt at a single conversation, and Sophie already had him wrapped around her little finger.

Damn, he really was screwed. And not in the good way.

After pulling on fresh clothes, he walked into the library to find it empty. Scowling, he headed downstairs and found Sophie in the middle of a mad rush, all the Guardian mates running amok doing small things. Packing, looking for important items, taking books from the downstairs library.

"What's going on?" he asked.

"You need to crash out for a few hours," Kieran said,

looking him up and down critically. "You look like you're dead on your feet."

"I've had much worse," Ephraim said with a shrug. "Why is everyone packing?"

"Sending the mates to a bolt-hole in the Gray Market. The Manor won't be secure enough, the wards have been defeated before," Aeric said. "Alice is in a panic, wanting to take every single dress she owns. I'm just standing back and letting the whirlwind happen."

After talking to Rhys and Aeric about patrol shifts for the next few days, Ephraim went to find Sophie where she was stuffing a pile of clothes in a suitcase, struggling to zip it.

"Here," he said, reaching out and holding down the top for her.

"Thanks," she said, flashing him a lopsided, grateful smile.

"How do you have this much stuff here already?" He asked, confused. "You just got here."

She chuckled.

"This isn't mine, it's…" she looked around. "Is it Echo? Yeah, it's hers. I do have a mysterious closetful of clothes and shoes that fit me perfectly in the bedroom next to yours, but I'm not going to the Gray Market."

"No?" Ephraim asked, mildly amused by the bossy tone in her voice. For such a little thing, she believed quite wholeheartedly in the power of her authority.

Then he thought about her holding up the keys that first night, and the smile slipped away.

She gave him an odd look, as if trying to guess his

thoughts. *Good luck with that one*, was his first. *I barely know my own thoughts these days.*

"I'm here to take down Papa Aguiel, not to hide out like Jesse James," she said. "I'm sticking with you."

"I've been wading through waves of zombies, possessed humans, and aggressive Vampyres taking advantage of the melee. No offense, but you're not going to be a lot of help unless you have some secret battle training I don't know about."

Her eyes sparked for a moment, but she didn't argue that point.

"We can hide out on our own then," she said, her eyes dropping to her feet. She was blushing again, but it didn't seem lust-induced this time.

It seemed more like she was hiding something, and doing a shit job at it.

"Is that right? Where will we go, Sophie?"

"I'm not sure…"

She glanced up at him, their gazes catching, electricity arcing between them. He realized it was the first time he'd called her by her name. It felt nice on his lips, made him wish he was saying it about an octave lower, while he held her down and fed her his…

Whoa, down boy.

Now Sophie was blushing in a physical way, and damn if Ephraim didn't want more.

"My *maladh*," he blurted, the words out of his mouth before he could stop himself.

"I'm sorry?" She asked, her brows rising.

"It means haven, safe place. My haven, my…" he trailed

off. "People think of it as a lamp, you know? Where I go when I am not being summoned."

Sophie gave him a soft smile.

"You'd take me there?" She asked, as if he'd just paid her the biggest compliment in the world.

And in a way, he had. He'd never taken anyone there, even in the direst of circumstances. It truly was his sanctum, a place where he could while away the endless hours of his life and forget the things he did for his masters in the outside world.

"I'd like that," she said. There was something in her eyes, something that made Ephraim feel a twinge of worry... but it was gone just like that, probably nothing more than his imagination.

Her lips curved up once more, and she reached out to brush a lock of hair back from Ephraim's face, the gesture making his heart pound.

"You look so tired," she said. "You need to rest."

Ephraim looked around at the Guardians, all in the midst of their preparations.

"I doubt we would be missed if we went to my *maladh* now," he said with a shrug. "I have the next full day off patrol."

Unable to help himself, he held out a hand to her.

"Just like that?" She asked.

"What more need there be?" Ephraim asked.

She gave him a heart-melting grin, her eyes shining for a moment, then slipped her small hand into his. Just that quick, Ephraim shifted them from the human plane to his maladh, a sort of bolt-hole between worlds. Accessible only to Ephraim, it was home, his castle, his oasis.

"Holy *crap*," Sophie breathed, staring up into the cavernous main room of his home.

The whole place was done up like a desert palace, soft beige inside and out. The maladh had many rooms, but this main living and sleeping area and the oversized spa bathroom were Ephraim's favorite.

Already Sophie was moving to the broad openings cut in the sides of the room. Because this was his private world, he made the rules, and here he could have massive open windows without worrying about the room growing hot or sandy.

Outside, the sun beat down on endless sand dunes, a vast stretch of nothingness beyond the huge swimming pool and grove of trees next to the house. There was nothing else in the world here, because he needed nothing else. The maladh fed him, clothed him, took care of all his basic needs.

In some ways, it was Ephraim's only friend, the only thing in his life that didn't demand anything from him in return. After all, the maladh did not keep him in servitude.

No, that was only every human and Kith he'd ever met.

Ephraim rubbed a hand over his face, his weariness making him feel overemotional and melodramatic.

"I'm going for a swim before I rest," he told Sophie. He needed to clear his head. "Make yourself comfortable, okay?"

He didn't wait for a response, heading down a grand sandstone staircase and tugging his shirt off as he went. He stripped down to his boxer briefs, uncaring whether

Sophie got an eyeful or not. He was overwhelmed and raw right now, he couldn't worry about her right now.

Shouldn't worry about her at all, in fact. Therein lay the problem.

The water was the perfect temperature when he dove in, just this side of refreshing. The sun had warmed the top and left the deeper recesses crisp and cool, and just the feel of the water on his skin was like sucking in a lifesaving breath just when he felt he was drowning.

He did a dozen laps, slow and methodical, the exercise burning his tired muscles but acting as a balm for his overwrought mind. It was meditative for him, and he slipped so far into his own world that the sound of splashing water jolted him mid-stroke.

Ephraim surfaced to find Sophie wading in, wearing what looked like nothing but one of his t-shirts. The thin cotton was already damp around her breasts and hips, clinging to the slick outlines of her curves.

There went his meditative state. His whole body tightened, cock growing hard in an instant as he watched her approach. She gave him a self-conscious smile and dove under the surface, swimming over to come up just a few feet from him, treading water.

"Sophie..." he warned. "I don't think you want to come any closer. I'm on edge right now."

"No, really?" She asked, rolling her eyes. "It's not really hard to tell, Ephraim."

Just hearing her say the word hard, and then hearing his name on her lips... Ephraim was dying, he was so damn hungry for her all the sudden.

Out of the thousands of times he'd fucked, out of the

countless acts of pleasure he'd performed, he could count on one hand the ones he'd truly *desired*.

Here she was, though, running her hands through her long, wet hair. She dove under the water, moving around, and when she came back up she held the t-shirt she'd worn in a hand.

The rest of her was completely, blissfully bare.

"Fuck," he muttered, already moving toward her.

He reached out and dragged her to his body, groaning when her full, bare breasts crushed against his chest, when her hot core pressed against his abs, when her sleek legs wrapped around his waist. He could have come just from that, like a horny teenaged boy. She was that sexy and irresistible to him.

"Ephraim," she whispered as he sought her soft lips, kissing her long and hard as he carried her toward the side of the pool. He snared her lower lip with his teeth, sucked on it. Explored her with his tongue, trying to hold in the hungry sounds filling his throat as he tasted her for the first time. Cupped her perfect ass with both hands, ran his thumbs over her hip bones.

It wasn't enough, not nearly enough.

When her ass hit the side of the pool, he leaned her back. Tugging her hair gently, he bowed her back until she thrust those magnificent breasts up at him, wanting. Her sex was slick and hot against him, her hips rocking in a gentle rhythm that threatened to burn him alive.

Fuck, he wanted to be inside her so bad.

Instead, he shaped both creamy mounds of her breasts and took his time exploring their curves, sucking and nibbling at her nipples until she was begging with need.

"Ephraim, *please*," she chanted. "Please, please, please."

"I know what you want," he whispered as he kissed her lips again. "I'm going to give you what you need, Sophie."

He lay her all the way back, parting her thighs easily and dropping down to kiss and tease her belly, her hips, her inner thighs. Her fingers drove into his hair, pulling tightly.

He froze for a moment, reaching up to gently remove her hands. He'd been pulled and forced enough in his life. Just this once, he wanted to be unbridled, to give her pleasure in just the way he wished.

When he found her clit with his lips and tongue, she cried his name, her thighs shaking with her need. Ephraim recognized in her what he often did in himself, the lack of touch and tender care.

No longer, not today. Not for his gorgeous Sophie.

When she was panting and writhing, soaking his lips and face with her need, he slid two thick fingers deep into her core. She shattered, convulsing and screaming her release to the heavens. He kept her going as long as he could, wringing every drop of pleasure from her body until she quieted and pulled at him, seeking his kiss on her mouth once more.

This time their kiss was slower, but no less intense and hungry. Ephraim's cock throbbed with his desire to fill her, complete their bond. She would be amazing, life-changing. Of that he had no doubt.

When was the last time Ephraim had fucked someone of his own volition, because *he* wanted to do so?

He had no idea.

Sophie's breathing grew faster again as she slid her

hand down between them, slipping under his wet boxer briefs to close her fingers around the steel length of his cock. Ephraim had to bite his lip to hold in the shout threatening to pour from his throat as she explored him with a gentle touch, nearly drawing his release with a few simple strokes.

In the perfectly wrong moment, his rational mind decided to intercede. Even as Sophie was rubbing her thumb just under the crown of his cock, burning him alive from the inside out, his brain flashed an image that he couldn't ignore.

Ephraim, buried balls-deep in Sophie. Sophie, wrapped around him, crying his name. And there, in her hand, the keys.

Ephraim stilled.

"No." It tore free from somewhere deep inside him, painful and angry and pure.

"W...what?" Sophie asked, her big blue eyes opening, nose scrunching in confusion. "No, what?"

"I can't," Ephraim said, pulling her hands away and stepping back. "This... this is for my true mate. I've waited a thousand years, and I'd wait a thousand more rather than do whatever... this is."

"Ephraim," she said, her brows knitting. "Let me... soothe you."

"No. Unless that's a command?" he spat, anger at her and at himself quickly flaring high.

"No! No, of course not," she said, looking hurt and horrified. "I wouldn't..."

Ephraim snorted.

"Wouldn't command me? Wouldn't act as my master? I

don't see you trying to set me free, Sophie. You're just like the rest of them, like every other owner I've ever had."

He could see that his words had found their target, see the pain in Sophie's eyes.

Good. He shouldn't be the only one hurting.

Turning, he left her there, seeking nothing more than his bed and the blissful darkness of sleep.

CHAPTER 6

Sophie stood on the far side of Ephraim's open bedroom, watching him sleep. He seemed to be deeply unconscious, not anywhere close to waking. She sucked in a quiet breath and looked around, knowing that if she was ever going to explore, this was the time.

She found several surprising things in her search. A room full of gilded treasure, something straight out of a Tolkien description of a dragon's hoard. A room of carefully preserved garments seemingly chronologically arranged, presumably Ephraim's own clothes through the ages. A windowless room with black walls and thousands of photographs, a timeline of Ephraim's life, his face appearing in the photos again and again in different scenes.

She had the distinct feeling that she was trespassing when she saw some of the more private moments, photos of Ephraim bound and strapped to BDSM crosses, photos of people dangling the keys over his prone form, photos of him in graphically sexual situations.

How had he even come to have these photos? Better question, what kind of fucked up life had Ephraim lived? Or since his powers seemed to be some kind of servitude, what had he been forced into?

Thinking of the moment at the pool when he refused her attentions, Sophie thought she understood a little better. Moreover, she knew a moment of distinct shame. If the kind of treatment depicted in these photos was all Ephraim knew, no wonder he didn't want to share himself with anyone in that way.

For all he knew, Sophie was no better than the rest of his owners.

Maybe I'm not, she thought to herself.

He wasn't one to forget his past, apparently. Sophie walked up and examined the photos close up, noting the vast and beautiful landscapes in the backgrounds, the glittering and gorgeous people in the photos with him. No matter the scenario, there was one constant: Ephraim looked passive, angry, stifled.

Never happy, not in one single photograph. She wrinkled her nose, trying to think if he'd ever smiled at her, a genuine and true smile.

Nope. Not once, ever.

She had to drag herself out of that room, curiosity eating her up. Ephraim was such a mystery to her, though his past was clearly tragic. The more she considered what it must have been like to be owned, the more she thought about the kind of person who would go out of their way to *own* another being... the more petals unfurled in the story of Ephraim.

And now Sophie herself was one of those people. *Fuck.*

She wandered the maze of his house, lost in thought, until at last she came to a hallway of closed doors. The hallway stretched on and on, out of her line of sight. For all she knew, it might truly be endless.

Something in her gut told her that this was where she needed to be. Glancing back over her shoulder, she stepped forward and opened the first door on her left. A sucking black void drew at her clothes, her hair, tugging her like a gentle vacuum.

"Shit!" she said, slamming the door closed. She let out a shaky laugh. "I guess that was to be expected."

"Not a particularly humanoid-friendly plane," came Ephraim's deep voice from behind her.

Sophie jumped and turned, guilt flooding her veins.

"Um, hey. You're up," was all she could manage. *And fully dressed*, Sophie thought with regret.

Ephraim watched her for a moment, then moved forward and grasped her wrist, pulling her out of the hallway and dangerously close to being in his arms.

"Why are you opening doors, Sophie?" he asked, his voice deadly-soft. He stared down at her, his eyes flashing that eerie yellow-green.

When Sophie's tongue darted out to wet her lower lip, his gaze dropped to her mouth for the barest moment. His jaw tensed and his grip on her wrist tightened.

"I was bored," she lied, her chin raising in defiance.

He looked down at her mouth a final time before releasing her, looking not a bit convinced.

"Those are all doors to other planes," he said, turning and moving back toward the main room, leaving Sophie to trail after him. "Open the wrong one… you're dead."

Though she knew he wasn't making a threat so much as stating a fact, the ice in his tone gave her a chill. Such distrust in every word he spoke, in every glance... no matter how heated.

The worst part was that she deserved that, on some level. Yeah, she was going to save a hell of a lot of lives and possibly the city by enacting her plan. But she was doing it to save her sister, not just out of the goodness of her heart.

"Is the spirit realm behind one of those doors?" she asked, before she could lose her nerve.

He faltered for a moment, then turned to stare at her.

"Why would you ask that?" He demanded to know.

"There are endless doors, endless planes of existence..." she waved her hand at the hallway. "It's got to be in there somewhere."

His gaze narrowed.

"It's the first door on the right, as a matter of fact," he snapped, shocking her with the immediate answer. "But you can't just waltz in there. It *changes* you."

The way he said it indicated that he knew from experience, but he wasn't exactly waiting around for Sophie's response.

"I shouldn't have brought you here. This was a mistake," he said, spinning and striding toward the main room once more.

"Ephraim, wait. I'm sorry," Sophie said. She hurried to keep pace with him.

"Sorry for what? For having secrets? For going through my private things without asking?"

At Sophie's look of surprise, he gave a sharp shake of his head.

"You think there's anything in this plane that happens without my knowledge? No. I hope you enjoyed playing the voyeur, Sophie. You wouldn't be the first of my masters who liked that kind of thing."

"Hey!" She said as they reached the main room. She turned the tables on him, reaching out and grabbing his hand to halt his movement. "Look at me."

"Sophie, there's nothing else that needs to be said," Ephraim said.

When she didn't let go, he turned back her with a soft sigh.

"I don't want..." she started, then stopped, biting her lip. What exactly was she trying to say, here?

"You don't know what you want, Sophie," he said, extracting his hand from hers.

"I want a lot of things, Ephraim." Her voice hardened when she thought of Lily; of course her greatest wish would be to get her sister back. "Things I can never have, things I don't have the strength to fight for. But I know this... I don't want to be like... like those people in your photographs."

The hurt and anger in Ephraim's eyes was like a punch to the gut. He seemed about to respond, then just shook his head and thrust his hand out to her again.

"We have to go back to the Manor."

"I thought you were taking the full day off to rest," Sophie said, taking his hand.

In a flash, they were back at the Manor.

"Yeah, well. I've had enough *rest* for one day," he said. "Besides, you didn't see how bad it was out there. I think a lot of the humans have already fled, but where will the Kith go? It's not like werewolves and Vampyres have extended family across the Gulf South to take them in."

Sophie just nodded, looking around the Manor's deserted living room.

"Awfully quiet in here," she said, just as the butler appeared, still dressed in his tuxedo, perfectly pressed.

"Duverjay," Ephraim said with a nod. "I'm back to resume patrols."

"I was hoping you were Rhys and Gabriel," the man said unapologetically. "They haven't checked in for some hours, though I expect that might just mean a dead cell phone battery."

Duverjay turned and paced to the kitchen island, drawing Sophie's attention to the massive arsenal of firearms he'd laid out there.

"Damn," she said. "Just what are you expecting, exactly?"

"There's a war raging outside, Kith against Kith. Possessed humans are turning up in droves, Vampyres too. Most of the shifters have headed for the hills, but there are plenty of demons and other evildoers lurking. I want to take as many out as I can from afar before I get pulled into combat," he said, rechecking the slide on one of his pistols.

"I see," Sophie said.

The butler gave a soft laugh, shaking her head.

"I doubt that very much. I'm a Berserker, long since

retired from the battle field. If I get drawn into what's happening out there, it's a last recourse. There are too many of them and not enough of us, and my bear doesn't know the meaning of the word *stop*."

"You'd fight to the death?" Sophie asked, pressing a hand to her heart.

"Without a moment's hesitation. I just want to make it count, you see. I plan to leave the Manor soon, head down and act as extra protection for the Guardians' mates. I've become quite attached to them all in my time here, and… well, I plan to be with them as long as I can. As long as they'll have me," he explained, grabbing a big duffel bag from one of the couches. "I'm loading myself up now. Is there anything I can get you two first?"

Ephraim shook his head solemnly, and Sophie followed suit.

The sound of the Manor's heavy front door opening and slamming closed made them all visibly tense; to Sophie's relief it was only Aeric, the big blond guy she'd met briefly yesterday.

"It's a shit storm out there," he said, shaking his head and throwing aside a sword that was missing at least a third of its length.

"Rhys has called all of the Louisiana Shifters in for help, but they only made it as far as the outskirts of the city before they got caught up in a battle," Duverjay informed Aeric.

"Damn," Aeric said, shaking his head. "Never in my life have I missed my dragon so."

"You're a dragon?" Sophie asked, awestruck. "I thought dragons were extinct!"

Aeric's lips twitched.

"I was a dragon," he corrected her. "No time for the story now, I'm afraid. Not with all the melee outside."

"We have to kill Papa Aguiel," Sophie said, crossing her arms. "It's that simple."

"Is it, now?" Aeric asked, eyeing her. "Have you got some kind of great plan then, mm?"

Sophie flushed. She did, but it wasn't as if she could tell *him* that. "Not that I can share, but I have been setting things in motion to see to his downfall, I assure you."

A strange expression flickered across Ephraim's face, a kind of sudden understanding. It took Sophie a minute, but she realized that Ephraim probably thought she was going to send *him* up against Papa Aguiel.

Before she could correct him, he was following Aeric toward the armory.

"Ephraim, wait!" she said, rushing to keep up.

"Go with Duverjay," Ephraim said, refusing to meet her gaze. "I will meet you back here tomorrow. Stay with the Guardians' mates tonight, help protect them."

He was trying to flatter her with that last bit, and she wasn't having any of it.

"Ephraim, no," she said, snagging his shirt sleeve. "You can't just... go off."

"Is that a command?" he asked, arching an imperious brow.

"No... but what if something happens to you before..." she stopped and bit her lip.

"Before what, exactly?" he asked, pulling his sleeve from her grasp and crossing his arms.

"I don't want to go to the Gray Market. I want to stay

with you," Sophie said, aware that she sounded like a whiny female. "I don't... I don't want to get separated."

That much was true, at least.

Ephraim softened, which made her feel guilty for the thousandth time in the past few hours. He reached out and squeezed her shoulders, drawing her close for a brief hug.

God, he smells so good, the dumb part of her brain said.

"I have to go, but I'll see you tomorrow night. Just go be with the other girls, okay? I don't want to have to worry about your safety," he said. After a moment's hesitation, he leaned down and brushed a burning kiss over her lips. "Be safe."

He turned and stalked off without a backward glance, leaving Sophie with a heartsick sensation in her chest and a thousand questions in her mind.

First and foremost: the way she felt right now, the way Ephraim was making her feel...

Was it fear for her plan, or for the man she was growing to like and respect? Was this just the mating attraction, that impossible-to-ignore hunger, or was it something more?

Greater than lust, stronger than simple need...

What was that called, exactly?

She shook her head, refusing to take that thought any further. She was a woman on a mission, not a lovesick schoolgirl. Just because he was handsome and had a storied past that spoke to her... Just because her body tightened every time she thought of the way he'd given her pleasure in the pool the night before... Just because she sensed his innermost goodness, trapped beneath all that sadness and anger, and a part of her desperately wanted to salve his wounds...

That didn't mean anything, right?

CHAPTER 7

*E*phraim was weary as death. Though reinforcements had slowly begun to filter in from around the world in the last week, it seemed that there was no turning back the tides. New Orleans was a ghost town, eerily vacant of meaningful life. And around every corner, hanging from every French Quarter balcony, was some hellish creature from beyond the Veil, lying in wait for the Guardians.

Aeric had relieved him on patrol over an hour ago, but the sheer effort of getting from one side of town to the other with all his body parts intact had nearly driven Ephraim to despair. Papa Aguiel was stirring up trouble all over town, threatening the precious few stubborn Kith and foolish humans that'd stayed behind.

It was all over the human news now, explained as "the outbreak of an unknown virus", something straight out of a bad zombie horror flick. Except this was real, and the virus was demonic possession. Oh, and there were also real bodies, dragged up from who knew where, to stagger about the city attacking anything in their wake.

He'd done the first two days straight through, and after that he'd been forced to start taking two or three short rests in each twenty four hour period. By day eight, today, he knew he needed a full measure of sleep in a real bed.

He also needed to check in on Sophie. The last time he was able to drop in on the Guardians' mates bolt-hole in the Gray Market, she was sound asleep. So now it had been a few days since he last talked to her.

It was torture, knowing he was cosmically assigned to her, that he was supposed to be her protector... in the midst of all *this*. Logically, he shouldn't care. She was gorgeous and compelling, yes. But her eyes spoke of secrets, and not the kind best left in the distant past.

She was hiding something from him, he just couldn't put together what it could possibly be. Something to do with her past and family? She evaded questions about both topics masterfully.

Or was it to do with her vendetta against Papa Aguiel? It was all she seemed to talk about, in between bouts of staring broodingly at Ephraim.

On one hand, he should be glad to be free of whatever schemes she was undoubtedly involved in. On the other hand... he liked being around her.

Liked the way she smelled, the way a smile could curve her lips. The first night he'd returned to the bolt-hole in the Gray Market to sleep, he'd awoken to find her curled around his body as he rested on a simple army cot. The feel of her body pressed against his, her warmth, the peaceful look on her face as she slept...

He couldn't get it out of his damn head. It had distracted him in battle several times, once in particular almost costing him what would've been a fatal blow to the neck.

Yep. He had it pretty bad for her. Maybe if he'd just taken what she'd offered so freely back at his *maladh*...

It wouldn't have been enough, though, and he knew it. Just the taste of her he'd gotten had nearly burned him alive, and his damn body wasn't about to let him forget it. He relived it in his dreams, as he showered, as he ran his sword through foes.

Yeah, he had a problem.

He turned a corner in the Gray Market, coming up on the highly-protected lair where the Guardians were stashing their ladies. He slowed, a familiar voice catching his attention. He stopped and backtracked, then peered around another corner. His shifter's vision allowed him to see the scene taking place in the shadowed alleyway, though a little part of him wished he couldn't.

Sophie stood across from a robed figure, nodding at something the other person said. She stuck her hand in her pocket and pulled out a sheaf of bills — an exorbitant amount of money, it looked like — and handed it over.

The other person thrust a dark, cloth-wrapped bundle at her. She grabbed it and tucked it under her arm, cradling it like something precious. She nodded once more at her mysterious companion, who turned and departed in the other direction. Sophie walked straight toward Ephraim, hardly looking up and certainly unaware of his presence.

Ephraim was about to step out and take her to task for leaving the safety of the bolt-hole, but a different kind of danger interceded.

With a definitive, hungry hiss, a trio of Vampyres descended from above, dropping to the ground and forming a tight circle around Sophie. He heard her mutter a curse, but she didn't drop the cloth bundle. Instead, she raised her hands and began to summon a bright orange blaze of power.

She was too slow. Sophie seemed to know it, and watching her realize it made Ephraim's heart skip more than a beat. Letting his sword fall to the cobblestone street with a clatter, Ephraim dropped to all fours and let his bear form take over.

All the bear knew, all it understood was the fervent, wild need to protect his mate. Ephraim gave him free reign, trying not to enjoy the shock on Sophie's face when a massive Grizzly bore down on her in the alley and proceeded to rip her foes apart.

Even better was her expression when he shook off the gore from the fight and shifted back to his djinn form. Her mouth was open in a perfect *o* of surprise that he found far too charming.

"You weren't supposed to leave the bolt-hole," he said, crossing his arms.

For once, Sophie seemed too flustered to respond.

"Let's go," he said, grabbing her by the elbow and towing her out of the alley. After reclaiming his sword from the ground, he marched her straight to the bolt-hole, past the common areas where the mates were gathered and into the private bedroom set aside for Sophie's use.

"Let's see it," he said, dragging off his heavy boots and collapsing on a chair beside the oversized bed.

"Ephraim—"

"Sophie, don't. You have no idea how tired I am right now. Don't make this another fight, please."

He sat back and folded his arms, eyeing the bundle of black cloth. When she huffed out a sigh and sank onto the bed opposite him, he knew he'd won this round.

"You're not going to like it," she told him point-blank.

"I like secrets even less," he said with a shrug.

She flushed, shaking her head so that her blonde hair rippled around her like a waterfall. Then she unwrapped the bundle and held out the gleaming, precious gem that laid inside. It was dazzling, bigger and brighter than any other Ephraim had ever seen in his long life.

And it was also *black*. Sickly, gleaming black that drew at him like a magnet. Before he realized it, he was reaching out with shaking fingers to touch it.

"No no no!" Sophie said, quickly covering it. "It's a soul stealer. One use only, and you are definitely not my intended target."

"I get the feeling that I don't want to know where or how you came to possess that thing," Ephraim said, rubbing a hand over his face.

"Correct. You wouldn't like the story, I guarantee it."

He sighed.

"You really are so much trouble," he told her, chuckling when she had the nerve to look offended. "Can you deny that?"

She bit her lip and shrugged.

"I don't mean to be," was all she would say.

"You know you can't use that, right?" Ephraim said. "I hate to be the bearer of bad news, but that thing is far, far too dark. Using something like that would… I don't even know what it would do to your soul, your aura."

"I don't see how you get a say in the matter," she said, her lips thinning.

She stood and carried the jewel over to the closet, setting it on a high shelf and closing the door on it. Then she paced back to where Ephraim sat, looking down at him imperiously.

"You're my mate," he said, narrowing his gaze on her face.

She laughed, a bitter sound.

"You're just some… person… I find attractive," she said, blushing at the last. "Neither of us is willing to go through with anything more than that, not with this kind of chaos in the city. And the chaos isn't going to end until…"

She waved her hand at the closet.

Ephraim reached out and closed his fingers around her wrist, tugging her nearer. She lost her balance and toppled into his lap, a pleasant surprise. Her big blue eyes went wide at the close contact, her tongue darting out to wet her bottom lip, just inches from his own.

"Why is this so important to you, hmm?" He asked. "I thought you would surely use me to do it, but now I think you want to do it yourself. It's personal, I can tell. What happened that would make you willing to risk your own soul for revenge?"

She bit her lip and glanced away.

"He hurt someone... someone I loved," she said. Tears shimmered in her eyes.

Jealousy rose in Ephraim's throat, hot and heavy.

"A man? A mate?" He asked. He reached out and turned her face back to his, staring straight in her eyes.

"No," she sputtered, her expression going dark. "Not a mate. And I'm not saying any more than that, so you can just drop it."

Relief filled him, making him realize just how strong his desire for Sophie really was.

"I need something from you," he said, struggling not to crush her against his chest and cover her lips in a demanding kiss.

"What?" She asked, her voice the barest whisper.

"If you're going to send me into an impossible battle... I'm not afraid to die, Sophie. I just don't want my last act to be an order, master commanding slave. Whatever you need of me, I will give it. Please just... ask."

A single tear welled up and rolled down her cheek. He could already see the denial on her lips, and he couldn't let her speak it aloud.

"You're the only mate I'll ever know, Sophie. Please don't take that from me. I will do anything for you, I swear. Anything."

Sophie closed her eyes for a moment, struggling with something.

"I would never send you up against Papa Aguiel," she said, opening her eyes after a long beat. "I told you already, I am the one who will defeat him."

"What, then? Why go to all the trouble to procure my

keys? You must need me for something," he said, searching her face and finding no answers.

Another tear rolled down her face, and Sophie brushed it away.

"Ephraim?" she asked. "I won't command it, but... will you take me to bed? Your bed, in your haven. It might..." her voice broke, and with it a little of Ephraim's heart broke as well. "It might be our last chance, our last night together."

Ephraim couldn't resist her entreaty, not when strong, stubborn Sophie looked at him with those big, tear-filled blue eyes.

Wrapping his arms around her, he vanished them both to his *maladh*.

CHAPTER 8

Sophie sighed as Ephraim carried her into his *maladh*, walking her over to a low plush couch. He sat her down and then stepped back, cocking his head.

"I think we should talk first," he said. "And I think that will require some bourbon."

He held up a finger, vanishing into some back room. Sophie fidgeted, uncomfortable. He wanted answers, that much was clear... and she wanted to give them to him.

The ones that wouldn't put him in danger, at least.

The attraction between them was too strong to deny. Again, she had the bitter thought that if they'd only met before Lily's disappearance, their entire relationship would be so different.

And it was a relationship, no matter what she wanted to tell herself. One glance at Ephraim made her blush; when their eyes met, she felt the desperate need to kiss him, to tell him every single thing on her mind.

He returned with two glasses of amber liquid, handing one over. Sitting beside her on the couch, he was enticingly close, their thighs brushing whenever one or the other moved.

"How do you even know that I like whisky?" she asked with a smile.

He shrugged.

"You don't seem like the wine cooler type."

They sipped in silence for several long moments, Ephraim raising a hand to magically dim the lights a little. He winked and said he was *setting the mood*. He reclined and watched her quietly, patient as ever.

"So? Aren't you supposed to start?" She asked, the whisky warming her insides in a pleasant way.

"I think you know what I'm going to say. I said it before," he sighed. "I want you, I know you can tell. I want nothing more than to drag you over to my bed right now. But I don't want you to use me. I don't want you to let me… feel things for you… and then turn around and treat me like your slave tomorrow. I only want to give myself to my mate."

Sophie bit her lip.

"I would never treat you like a slave," she said.

"Giving me commands, flashing the keys at me to assure my compliance," he said, ticking off items on his fingers. "Guess what that feels like? Knowing that you need me for something, but not knowing what you're going use me for… that's not mate behavior, no matter how much I want you."

She nodded slowly.

"What if… what if I can promise you that I'm not going to send you into anything dangerous? What if I promise that you've already provided me what I really need?"

Ephraim's brows shot up.

"Is that right?" He said. She could see the gears working in his head, see him trying to figure that out.

She wrinkled her nose, running the words through her head again to make sure they were true, then nodded. She set her glass aside, giving in to the urge to move a little closer, resting a hand on his arm.

"If I ask you for anything else, it wouldn't be more than what you've already done for me." She paused for a second, leaning a little closer to Ephraim. "Would that be enough assurance for you, if I gave you my word I'd never use the keys against you?"

An unfathomable expression flickered across Ephraim's face. He didn't respond with words, but an irresistible smile appeared where his frown had been. He leaned closer, enveloping Sophie in his delicious, masculine smell.

"You promise?" He whispered, his gorgeous spring green eyes searing her.

Sophie let her eyes drift closed, leaning in and pressing her lips to his. One of her hands landed on Ephraim's chest, the other cupped his neck tenderly, her fingers tugging at the silky strands of his chin-length hair and drawing him closer.

The soft growl that rumbled from his throat excited her. She surged forward, wanting to be closer, wanting to feel the press of his hard chest against her breasts, the heat of his thighs against hers. She moved to climb on his lap, thinking to straddle him, but Ephraim surprised her by scooping her up and carrying her across the room to his bed.

He sprawled on the bed, gently trapping Sophie under his big body. Already she could feel the thick length of his cock through both their jeans, ready and waiting for her. Her hands plucked at his shirt, eager to strip him, feel his bare skin against hers.

She'd wanted this since the moment she laid eyes on Ephraim, wanted it more than anything else… thought of him, fantasized about this more than she'd thought of her current plans for revenge. It was an escape, no doubt, but with Ephraim she'd found something deeper than expected.

He captured both her hands and brought them up above her head, nipping at her lips as he carefully stripped off her thin white silk blouse. Then he freed her hands and tugged off her dark jeans, leaving her in nothing but a black lace bra and panties.

"Ephraim…" she said as he dropped teasing kisses on her ribs, her inner thighs.

"Let me take care of you, Sophie," he murmured against her skin. Cool air caressed her breasts as he slid her bra off, cupping and kissing each breast with infinite patience, tenderness, and hunger.

Each flick of his tongue, each warm press of his lips, each time his stubbled chin brushed her sensitive skin, she burned a little higher. Heat rippled outward from her chest, pooling low in her body and raising gooseflesh all over her skin.

"Ephraim," she said again, this time more urgently.

His lips curled into a smile as he kissed her navel, moving lower and yanking her panties down her legs. He caressed her legs as he spread her thighs, exploring her dampness with long, lazy licks of his hot tongue. When he closed his lips over her clit, Sophie writhed, too carried away with her hunger to be embarrassed by the brazen rocking of her hips.

Just as her body was tightening, her release moments away, he pulled back and favored her with a hungry look.

"Tease," she accused, biting her lip.

"I want to feel you come around me," he said, pulling up the hem of his shirt to take it off and tossing it aside, revealing miles of incredible, perfectly sculpted muscle.

"Damn, you are so sexy," she told him, reaching out and running her hands down his tanned chest, hooking her thumbs in the twin dips of muscle at each hip bone.

She looked up and met his gaze as she unbuttoned his jeans, undressing him with artful slowness. She dragged his tight navy boxer briefs off, sucking in a little breath of anticipation when she saw his full, naked glory.

He was *huge*. Long, thick, and perfect. Her fingers were encircling his girth before she knew it, exploring him in the same languid strokes he'd used to pleasure her with his tongue. She pushed him onto his back and straddled his legs, taking his length in her fist and leaning down to swirl her tongue around the thick crown.

"Sophie, *fuck*," he gritted out, brushing the hair back from her face. "You're killing me, I swear."

She gave him a mischievous smile before positioning herself to take him deeper, moaning with pleasure when he cried out her name again. Every muscle in his body stood in stark relief; Ephraim seemed to vibrate with his need for release.

All too soon, though, he was pulling her away.

"Damn if I'm going to spend in your throat, no matter how lovely this mouth might be," he said, his dirty talk making her blush. It was silly, given the intimacy of their positions, but Ephraim made her blood race in new and exciting ways.

Sophie let Ephraim drag her up his body, accepting his kiss as he positioned himself at her entrance. She sat up, letting her breasts thrust out, enjoying the look of male appreciation on his face. He lifted her, ready to bring their bodies together

He froze for a second.

"I... I haven't considered birth control in at least fifty years," he admitted, pulling her down so that he could nuzzle her neck, cup her breast absently.

"It's taken care of," Sophie said, kissing his lips, hungry for more of him. "Modern miracles of science and all."

"Thank the gods," he muttered, leaning up to give the tip of her breast an appreciative nip.

"Fuck me, already," Sophie said, giving him an answering bite on his lower lip.

He arched a brow but didn't protest, lifting her and bringing her core flush to the head of his cock. Just as he would have started to push in, he paused again.

"Mmm... wrong position," he said, an evil smile on his face.

Sophie opened her mouth to protest, but just that quickly Ephraim was flipping her over. Face down, ass up, knees spread wide. When he positioned himself and filled her in one deep, nerve-frying thrust, she cried out and clutched at the covers.

"Ephraim, yes!"

He gripped her hips hard as he thrust into her again and again, slowing to slap her ass cheek hard, and then picking up speed again. Sophie went over the edge of some unknowable sensation, her face pressed into the comforter. She knew nothing, saw nothing, had nothing in her life except the feeling of Ephraim as he worked her body hard.

Her breasts tightened to the point of near pain, her whole body felt heavy and full and needy. She was so, so close but she couldn't quite let go, not without him.

She wanted so, so badly to feel him lose control, feel him come in her. That thought alone almost pushed her to the breaking point, but she held on.

Her throat ached, but she couldn't hear her own cries of pleasure. When Ephraim's clever fingers slid around her hip and down her thigh, finding her clit, she shattered in an instant, clenching and screaming and sobbing.

Ephraim came with a shout, fingers gripping her hips painfully hard, pumping his seed deep inside her body again and again, fulfilling her fantasy in ways she couldn't have comprehended.

He shocked her then, wrapping an arm around her and pulling her up, pressing his lips to her neck. He buried his teeth in her neck, marking her as his mate, taking her by complete surprise.

She should fight, rail against him. She should be angry that he hadn't even *asked* whether she wanted it, wanted him…

Instead she allowed Ephraim to pull her down to the bed, to wrap her in his arms, to whisper sweet things against her neck where her new mating mark lay. Every other minute of every day, she fought.

Right here, right now...

Surrender was her escape, and Ephraim the fulfiller of her dreams.

Just for tonight...

Even as she thought the words, the bite on her neck ached, and she knew they weren't true. She was Ephraim's now, and Ephraim was hers. For better or for worse, they were bound... at least until Sophie managed to kill Papa Aguiel, which would probably destroy her completely.

Better not to think of that now. Better to inhale Ephraim's sultry, comforting scent, lay in his protective embrace, soak in his warmth...

And lie to herself, if that's what it took to snatch this one tiny bit of happiness.

CHAPTER 9

Bedlam didn't quite begin to describe the state of the French Quarter when Sophie and Ephraim rode down Decatur Street in the Guardians' armored SUV. Duverjay was driving all the males plus Alice and Echo, who were apparently allowed to go on such a dangerous mission. As they cruised past the French Market, paying absolutely no attention to the usual one-way streets, the place was deserted.

Except the staggering corpses and the possessed, who were legion in number. Groups of them moved in swarms, this direction and that, single-minded as flocks of sheep being herded onward… but to what?

"Shit, there are a bunch of humans running away from the Riverwalk," Aeric said, pointing toward the paved area where the French Quarter met the Mississippi river. "They don't look particularly possessed to me."

"Pull over," Rhys commanded Duverjay. "And don't you dare let Echo leave this truck."

Sophie arched a brow. So that was the deal Echo had worked out, getting out of the Gray Market but being forced to stay in the car? Raw deal, in Sophie's opinion.

Her own mate was looking at her like he wished nothing more than to force her to do the same, but he just stayed tense and silent. When the SUV screeched to a halt, they all piled out. Half the Guardians spread out toward the approaching humans, but it was a lost cause. After a few moments all the humans stopped dead, staring forward mindlessly.

"Papa Aguiel's got them under his spell all right," Ephraim said to Sophie. She nodded. In a terrifying moment, all the humans turned as one and began to stagger back toward the river.

"He's on the Steamboat Natchez," Sophie said, pointing at a bright bolt of blue light that rose into the night sky. "He's probably channeling raw elemental power straight from the river, using it to help bolster his control over the possessed."

Sticking her hand into her pocket, Sophie reassured herself that the thin velvet pouch holding the black gemstone was still there. Waiting for her, it seemed.

As she and Ephraim and the rest of the Guardians rushed to follow the possessed humans, Papa Aguiel made his presence more clear. Bolt after bolt of magic spewed into the sky, and a dark figure could be seen on the deck of the boat, swathed in the same blue light.

As Sophie racked her brain for desperate, last-minute brain storms on how she might use the gemstone on Papa Aguiel without involving Ephraim, her mate shifted into his bear form and barreled toward a large group of zombies that swept in from the east side.

Watching him fight, measuring the quarter-mile of foes and battles between the Guardians and Papa Aguiel, Sophie knew she had no choice. Yes, she might lose Ephraim forever if she used her powers of command against him. Yes, it would crush her; if using the soul stealer didn't wreck her aura permanently, driving Ephraim away would.

But if she didn't... she and Ephraim would both die, along with the rest of the city, perhaps eventually the world. Lily's spirit would be glommed to Papa Aguiel's for the duration, never free to move on to the next world.

As far as choices went, they were all hard as hell. But the idea of Lily's legacy being part of what would be the downfall of all humankind...

"Ephraim!" She shouted, trying to get his attention before she lost her nerve. Already cursing herself, she pulled the keys from her back pocket and held them high. "T-take me to your haven!"

The fury on his face was undeniable. He came over to her, his movements as still and jerky as those of the possessed she'd seen earlier. Tears running down her face, Sophie just stood there and waited for him, knowing she'd crushed the most special thing in her entirely shitty new life.

When Ephraim took her hand in a bruising grip, she didn't wince. She welcomed the pain. He closed his eyes and transported them from the battlefield in a moment's thought. Ephraim's quiet, ethereal *maladh* was a balm to her senses, but she wanted none of it.

"Don't go," Ephraim said through gritted teeth. "Whatever you're going to do, please don't. Sophie…"

"He killed my sister," Sophie told him. "Because she was innocent, he used her to gain a foothold into this world. Her spirit can never rest, because a piece of her rides along with him forever."

Ephraim turned away from her, but Sophie needed her final goodbye.

"Stay still," she commanded him.

His anger was almost palpable, but Sophie just walked around to slip her arms around his shoulders, giving him a tight hug. She pushed up onto her tiptoes to kiss his unyielding lips, unable to look him in the eye. His disgust was more than she could take, just now.

"I have to do this, alone. It's going to kill me, probably. I can't let you make that sacrifice, not for any reason," she told him. "I'm going down the hallway, into the spirit realm, and I am probably not coming back." She glanced up at him for the barest moment, only affirming the pure fire she saw in his gaze. "I wouldn't have anything or anyone to come back to anyway, not after this. On the upside, the keys will probably die with me. I think… I researched a little, and I think it might free you when my spirit dissipates."

She tucked the keys in her pocket, and turned to leave.

"Don't follow me. That's my last command. And Ephraim—" she glanced at him one last time, wiping away her tears, trying to be brave. "I'm sorry. You deserved so much better than me."

Sophie left him then, not stopping until she reached the hallway. After a deep, fortifying breath, she yanked open the door to the spirit realm and stepped inside, not stopping for so much as a backward glance.

This was her fate.

CHAPTER 10

*E*phraim stood frozen for several minutes, Sophie's command holding him so tightly that he couldn't even think to resist. He heard a door slam in the distance, knew she'd gone through the portal to the spirit realm. His muscles locked him in place, but his mind began to relax.

For a brief, guilty moment Ephraim considered just letting her go, waiting until the night's inevitable conclusion. If Sophie died in the spirit realm, there was some chance that she might indeed incidentally free him of his servitude.

But no. She was *his*, his mate. His to protect and cherish, his to save. He couldn't let her go on alone, no matter what it meant for him personally.

The second that the spell loosened enough for him to begin to move, he started to force himself to walk. Blinding, searing pain thundered through his veins, screamed agony in his mind, but he kept going. Far past his limit, ignoring what he *could* do and focusing instead on what he *must*.

Making it as far as the door took longer than he expected; opening it and stepping through into the spirit realm was unbearable. Shaking, he surged onward, trying to move faster. Mindless of all except his desperate need to get to *her*.

It felt like a lifetime, but eventually he found her standing at a sort of wall, if you could call it that. The wall was midnight blue, as high and wide as he could see. It was set with thousands, or maybe millions, of the finest points of white imaginable. Tiny, twinkling lights dancing against deep blue, like so many stars blanketing the night sky.

One single star stood out from the rest, hanging an arm's length above Sophie's head, burning a fiery blue.

"Sophie," he said, calling for her attention.

When she turned, startled, she seemed deflated.

"You're... here? But how?" She asked.

Her face was red and swollen from crying, and she clutched the cloth-covered jewel in both hands.

"I can resist commands. It's just... very, very painful," he admitted. "You're my mate, Sophie. We're bound together, no matter what. I couldn't let you come here alone."

Her shoulders sagged. If he'd expected jubilation on her part, he was to be disappointed.

"I release you," she said, shaking her head.

Instantly his pain evaporated, though his ears still rung ever-so-faintly.

"What is this?" He asked, stepping up to stand beside her.

"It took me a minute, too." She pursed her lips. "That blue light… that's Papa Aguiel. And all the rest of these…"

She waved her fingers to indicate the rest of the lights.

"All souls?" He asked, and she nodded.

"Has to be."

"Put that in your pocket for a second," Ephraim said, nodding to the stone she held.

When she did so, albeit slowly, Ephraim reached out and grabbed her by the waist. He shocked her by pulling her up against his body, hard. He took her lips in a demanding, hungry kiss and didn't release her again until they were both breathless and aching.

"That?" He said, resting his forehead against hers. "That's our bond, Sophie. You can't let me kill Papa Aguiel? Well, I can't let you do it, either. If we are fated mates, and I think there's no denying that by now. Our lives are supposed to become intertwined. Grow together, for the rest of our existence."

"Ephraim, I can't let you do it."

"What you said before, about how you won't have anything to go back to? If you do this, I won't either."

They stood like that for a minute, staring each other down. Sophie let out a shuddering breath and broke the gaze.

"Then we are at an impasse, Ephraim. What do you suggest I do?" She asked, her voice sad.

Reaching down, Ephraim linked his fingers with hers and raised her hand as he raised his own.

"We do it together. Whatever happens, it happens to both of us. Neither of us will be left behind."

A fresh tear tracked down Sophie's face.

"I really don't deserve you, Ephraim."

"We deserve each other," he said, giving his head a gentle shake. "I can see that now."

"What do you think will happen?" She asked, her words giving him hope.

"I can't say. Maybe… if we're very, very lucky, we could each take a little of the bad instead of a full dose… If not, wherever we go, at least we will be together."

She bit her lip, then pulled the gem from her pocket. Pulling back the black velvet pouch, she glanced up at him again.

"Are you sure?" she asked.

Ephraim nodded solemnly.

She dropped it into both their palms where Ephraim's fingers were laced with hers. Ephraim let out a grunt at the searing burn of the jewel on his flesh, but didn't flinch.

"Together," Sophie whispered.

They reached up, both jumping up to clap the jewel against the burning blue star in that endless midnight sky. To Ephraim's surprise, the jewel sucked at the star and the star sucked right black, pulling magic from a deep wellspring somewhere deep inside him.

Powering the spell.

Suddenly the jewel heated unbearably, and as Ephraim pulled Sophie backward from it, it shattered. Thousands of shards of darkness descended, covering them, raining down from above, filling Ephraim's consciousness with inky blackness.

The last thing he recognized was the feel of Sophie's palm, still pressed against his.

All else vanished.

CHAPTER 11

Sophie came to consciousness standing beside Ephraim in a world of dim, endless white. White mist billowed everywhere, clinging damply to Sophie's skin. It could have stretched for miles or ended just a few feet from Sophie's face, it was impossible to tell.

"Where are we?" Ephraim asked. His voice was hushed and distorted, as if he was speaking from a far distance.

Sophie shook her head, reaching out and taking the hand he offered. Lacing her fingers with his soothed her, made her feel grounded despite their surroundings.

"Do you think we died?" She asked after a moment.

Ephraim glanced at her, then shook his head.

"Don't think so."

"Do you see that?" Sophie said, pointing to their left. She squinted into the distance, thinking she could just make out... well, she wasn't sure what.

"Is that a tree?" Ephraim asked. "Let's go look."

Giving her hand a reassuring squeeze, he gently towed

her toward the indistinct shape. Sure enough, as they moved toward it, the mist cleared away. There was a single Japanese maple rising high in the air, its red leaves startling against the whiteness of the world. Next to it there was a small pond with a shoreline of perfectly round gray pebbles. Just beneath the tree was a finely wrought wooden bench, and on the bench sat a lone figure.

Even from this distance, even though the figure's shoulders were hunched, her nose nearly buried in a big green book, Sophie knew her at once.

"Lily," she gasped. "Ephraim, that's my sister."

Tears welled in her eyes at once. She didn't let Ephraim's hand go, instead dragging him along with her. When they got close enough for their footsteps to be noisy, Lily glanced up and gave them a wan smile. Closing her book, she sat it aside and stood, brushing off her simple white dress. Her long blonde hair was neatly braided, her cheeks pink.

"There you are," Lily said, as if this were all perfectly normal.

"Oh, Lily!" Sophie cried, releasing Ephraim at last and flinging herself into her sister's arms.

"Oh—" Lily tried to warn her, but Sophie's enthusiasm was too strong.

She stepped right through her sister's solid-looking but ultimately insubstantial body.

"Sorry," Lily said, pulling a face. "Nothing is... permanent... here. You won't be able to touch anything."

Sophie wrapped her arms around herself, trying to

hold in the sudden burst of sadness she felt at not being able to hold her sister. It was just that Lily was so close now... and yet, somehow, a world away.

"I miss you so bad, Lil. I just... it's been really tough without you," Sophie said slowly.

"I noticed. You weren't coping very well. I've been watching from here," Lily said. "It was hard to witness."

"I have so many questions. Mostly... are you okay here? Is it... it seems lonely," Sophie blurted out.

"Where are we?" Ephraim asked, clearing his throat.

Lily turned and favored him with a look.

"You must be my sister's mate," she said, tucking a piece of hair back behind her ear. She raised a brow at Sophie. "Handsome."

"Lily..." Sophie was at a genuine loss. "*Why* are we... wherever we are?"

"We are... let's say, *in between*. It's lonely here, sure, but there are tons of other people on the other side. When you two destroyed that horrible man, you freed the last piece of my soul, which Papa Aguiel tarnished quite badly. You also damaged your own souls in the process. So now we're all here, in between. This is where we will be cleansed, and then sent on our way."

"On our way to where, precisely?" Ephraim was quick to ask.

"Lily, are you saying you're coming back to the human realm with us? Or are we... are we going to the afterlife?" Sophie asked, her heart beginning to pound.

Lily gave her a sad smile.

"We're going in different directions. You're going

back," she said, pointing. When Sophie glanced to where Lily indicated, she could see the barest outline of a portal forming, glowing with a soft yellow light.

"And you?" Sophie asked.

Lily pointed again, in the opposite direction. "Forward," was her only explanation for a twin portal, this one glowing pink.

"Oh," Sophie said, her shoulders slumping.

"I was going to carry you forward with me," Lily said, cocking her head. "I didn't want you to be alone. But now... now, I couldn't. I can see that the two of you have very big things coming."

Tears slipped down Sophie's cheeks. She glanced at Ephraim, who moved to her side and took her hand again.

"We do," Ephraim affirmed. "Right, Sophie?"

Sophie nodded slowly, still looking at Lily with longing.

"Honestly? Time is so different here," Lily said, glancing around. "It'll be the blink of an eye for me, and then we'll all be together again."

"You sound pretty certain of that," Ephraim said, brows arching.

"I am," Lily said. She pursed her lips. "For now, though... you two take good care of one another. I'll be watching to make sure."

Both of the portals grew brighter and brighter, and Lily sighed.

"That's our cue," she said. "Do me a favor, though? Take this book with you, make sure Mere Marie gets it. She's going to need it."

She picked up the heavy leather-bound text and thrust it into Sophie's hands. Sophie was shocked at how heavy and real it was, after her experience trying to touch Lily.

"What is it?" She asked.

"Don't worry about it," Lily said, waving a hand. "Someone just asked me to pass it along."

Her form shimmered, growing transparent.

"Lily, I miss you so much," Sophie said.

"You too, Soph. Just go live the hell out of your life, enough for the both of us. I'll see you soon enough, I promise."

Lily gave her a last smile and then moved toward her portal. Sophie felt Ephraim gently pulling her in the opposite direction, and she let him guide her away. Lily vanished in a flash of pink, and soon Sophie was stepping through her own portal, the book clutched to her chest.

A gentle wash of pure white magic brushed over her as she went, and she could feel it stripping away the layers of dark magic, the results of her single-minded campaign against Papa Aguiel.

It was like taking a deep breath of the cleanest air possible, while plunging into crystal-cold water. Cleansing, purifying, and satisfying on a soul-deep level.

When Sophie and Ephraim landed back in the endless hallway of his maladh, she looked at him and smiled.

"Your aura... it's perfectly pure," she said.

"Yours, too. And I have another surprise," he said, raising a brow.

"Yeah?"

He took Sophie's hand and brought it to his neck. Her fingers met nothing but smooth, warm skin.

"Your collar's gone!" She said, astonished.

"You did that for me," he said, a slow smile growing on his lips.

"What? How?" She asked, color rising in her cheeks.

"Your greatest desire was to take down Papa Aguiel, *alone*. When you let me help you, you sacrificed that wish… and freed me in the process."

"Why didn't you say something before?" She asked, smacking him lightly on the arm.

"Oh, I don't know. Saving the world, seeing your sister's ghost… we had a lot going on," he joked.

"Oh, Ephraim," Sophie sighed. She set the book aside and threw her arms around him. She hugged him hard, trying not to cry for the hundredth time today. "What will we do now? We've been so wrapped up in trying to save the world, we haven't even had that discussion."

"You know what's amazing?" He said, stroking her hair.

"Hmm?"

"We can go anywhere, do anything. We know that we're fated mates, and that was the hard part. After all that fighting each other and trying not to die, we can just… be alone, figure each other out, decide what we want. We have an immortal lifetime to do all of that."

Sophie pulled back a little, glancing up at him. Tears were definitely pricking her eyes now, she couldn't help it.

"Yeah?" was all she could manage.

"Absolutely," he swore. "For now… I say we head back to the human realm, check on the Guardians. Don't forget, we have a mysterious book to deliver. How does that sound?"

"Couldn't be more perfect," Sophie agreed. "Let's go."

Lacing her fingers with Ephraim's, Sophie grinned. She'd go anywhere with him, do anything he wanted.

After all, he was her mate for life... forever and always.

EPILOGUE

"All right. I think I need to retire for the night," Mere Marie said with a regretful sigh. "After almost two days of celebrations, I'm tapped out. I'm too old for this."

They were all gathered in the kitchen, sipping St. Germain punch and swapping almost-the-end-of-the-world stories. Rhys and Gabriel both snorted, but Mere Marie just pointed to baby Marie, who was sleeping soundly on Cassie's shoulder.

"She's got the right idea," Mere Marie said, giving the baby a fond pat on the back.

"Tomorrow, we should talk business," Aeric said, stretching and setting his champagne flute aside. "Now that we've defeated our two biggest enemies, I'd like to imagine that the Guardians become sort of peacekeepers… instead of constantly trying to stop an apocalypse."

Mere Marie nodded.

"The Manor belongs to the Guardians and their families," she said, smiling at the sleeping baby again. "I hope as many of you stay here as possible, permanently."

"There's time to work all that out," Rhys said, emptying the last of his drink in a single sip.

"Actually... on that front, we have some news," Kira spoke up. "Now that things are calmer, Asher and I are going to take off for a while. Travel, see the world. We have a lot of catching up to do."

She reached down and took Asher's hand, and the adoring glance he gave Kira was so sweet it was nearly sickening. He kissed the top of her head and beamed at her, oblivious to all else.

"Well, as Rhys said. All things we can talk about tomorrow. For now, I think a good night's rest sounds great," Mere Marie said.

After a round of *goodnights*, she headed upstairs and got into her nightgown. She let down her long white hair and sat on the side of her bed, then nearly fainted with fright. The candles flickered, some of them going out.

The room turned chilly.

And there he was. Standing in the middle of her bedchamber, ghostly but all too present, was Le Medcin.

"Monsieur," she said, dipping her head in a respectful gesture and pressing her hand to her pounding heart. "You scared me."

He wore his usual finely-made but ancient-looking suit, the dove gray material making his ebony skin look even darker. Just looking at him fascinated and repulsed her, such was his power.

"You have done very well, Marie," he said, his deep voice spreading a chill of gooseflesh up her arms.

"Thank you, Monsieur." She waited, knowing he must be here for a reason.

"Your Guardians have been very successful, much more so than I anticipated. Still..." he paused for a moment. "The human world is in a very dangerous position. The war between Heaven and Hell, good and evil... The tide is turning, and not in our favor."

She was surprised to hear Le Medcin refer to himself as being on the side of good. Or any side, really... until this moment, she'd considered him to be a truly neutral force. The referee between good and evil, one might say.

"I see," was all she could think to say.

"You will need to put your affairs in order," he said, changing the topic. "In twenty four hours, you will meet your new charges."

"I— what?" She asked, confused.

"Come," he said, beckoning her over to the broad scrying mirror in the corner of her bedroom. Pressing a single ghostly finger to the mirror's surface, he caused it to ripple and shift, forming an image.

The angle of their view was odd, but after a moment it righted itself. Thick black steel bars formed a cage and obscured part of what she could see, but the occupants of the prison were clear as day.

Three hulking, muscular men. Covered in tattoos, fierce expressions of hatred on their faces. They stood, arms crossed, staring straight at Mere Marie as if they somehow knew she was watching.

Most extraordinary of all, each of the three men had a set of glorious wings, rising high above their heads.

"Angels," Mere Marie whispered, crossing herself without thought.

"Fallen angels," Le Medcin corrected her with a sigh. "These three have been… troublesome. We need someone to oversee them in the coming days. It is believed that they will be a key part of the forces of good, that which protects the human realm and keeps Lucifer himself from walking the Earth, taking dominion over each living soul in the world."

Mere Marie's mouth opened and closed again. She was rarely without words, but this… this was something else.

"The Devil is out there, Marie. And he's a lot bigger and meaner and smarter than the forces you've battled here. These three warriors I'm giving you… they would have made great Guardians, but now we need them for a higher purpose. Just like we need you for a higher purpose. Prepare yourself."

"But why now?" She couldn't help but ask.

Le Medcin watched her for a silent beat, seeming to consider how much to tell her.

"I cannot prove it, but Hell is tipping the scales somehow. We cannot allow them to continue. They will decimate the world, enslave all humans and Kith, rain fire from the skies."

"I… okay," was all she got out before he was talking again.

"One full day from now, I will summon you. Pack light, bring what you need."

He pressed a cream-colored business card into her hands, and she tried not to shudder at the icy touch of his flesh against hers. Then he was gone, vanished like the apparition he was.

She stared down at the card she clutched with shaking fingers.

"Les Mercenaires," she read aloud.

It sounded familiar....

Cairn's soft purr filled the room as he slipped in to twine around her feet. The black cat sat at her feet, looking up at her with his luminous eyes.

"Are you all right?" He asked softly.

"Start packing up all the important books," she told her familiar. "We leave tomorrow night."

"For how long?" He asked.

"I don't know."

"Where are we going?"

"I don't know."

"Well what do you know?"

She glanced down at the cat, a cool smile on her lips.

"I think our lives are about to get very interesting," she said, shrugging.

With that, Mere Marie turned and began preparing herself to meet her first fallen angel.

GET A FREE BOOK!

JOIN MY MAILING LIST TO BE THE FIRST TO KNOW OF NEW RELEASES, FREE BOOKS, SPECIAL PRICES AND OTHER AUTHOR GIVEAWAYS.

http://freeshifterromance.com

ALSO BY KAYLA GABRIEL

Alpha Guardians

See No Evil

Hear No Evil

Speak No Evil

Bear Risen

Bear Razed

Bear Reign

ABOUT THE AUTHOR

Kayla Gabriel lives in the wilds of Minnesota where she swears she sees shifters in the woods beyond her yard. Her favorite things in life are mini marshmallows, coffee and when people use their blinker.

Connect with Kayla by
email: kaylagabrielauthor@gmail.com and be sure to get her FREE book: freeshifterromance.com

http://kaylagabriel.com

www.ingramcontent.com/pod-product-compliance
Lightning Source LLC
LaVergne TN
LVHW011845060526
838200LV00054B/4169